"I've never shown anyone this place before."

The vulnerability she saw in Linc's expression tugged at her heart. "I'm honored. It's a beautiful location. It would be a lovely family estate."

"I've had plenty of offers to buy it. But I'll never sell."

"I can't blame you. Living here would be wonderful." Gemma slipped her hand into his, and he squeezed it gently, her breath catching with his gaze. There was a softness, a longing, as if he'd pulled back a curtain and allowed her to see something deeply personal.

"I wanted you to understand."

"Why?" Did he want her to care?

What if she made another mistake? What if Linc wasn't all he appeared to be?

No. She'd better douse this attraction with a bucket of common sense and keep her focus on the only things that really mattered. Evan and the Christmas events.

Then Linc smiled. Common sense vanished like morning mist in sunlight.

She was in big trouble. Big, big trouble.

Lorraine Beatty was raised in Columbus, Ohio, but now calls Mississippi home. She and her husband, Joe, have two sons and five grandchildren. Lorraine started writing in junior high and is a member of RWA and ACFW and a charter member and past president of Magnolia State Romance Writers. In her spare time she likes to work in her garden, travel and spend time with her family.

Books by Lorraine Beatty

Love Inspired

Home to Dover

Protecting the Widow's Heart
His Small-Town Family
Bachelor to the Rescue
Her Christmas Hero

Rekindled Romance
Restoring His Heart

Her
Christmas Hero

Lorraine Beatty

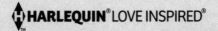

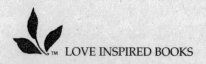

™ LOVE INSPIRED BOOKS

Recycling programs for this product may not exist in your area.

ISBN-13: 978-0-373-87995-3

Her Christmas Hero

www.Harlequin.com

Printed in U.S.A.

Chapter One

Linc Montgomery stepped out onto the front porch of his family home, inhaling the cool October air deep into his lungs. His gaze drifted over the green lawn that sloped to the tree line and beyond. The view never failed to siphon the tension from his body and soothe his soul. And he needed both right now. Leaning one shoulder against a fluted porch post, he prayed for strength to get through the day. The death of his father a month ago had shaken him to the core, and the grief at times was overwhelming.

He growled and exhaled a heavy sigh at the sound of an approaching car. He couldn't handle another well-wisher dropping off food that probably wouldn't get eaten. He appreciated their kindness and concern, but he didn't have it in him today to make nice. A nondescript domestic silver sedan appeared between the old oaks that lined the long winding driveway. He didn't recognize it. In a town the size of Dover, Mississippi, it was easy to identify a person by the car they drove.

Linc straightened and shoved his hands into the front pockets of his jeans, struggling to dig up a smile and a grateful attitude. The car drove past the main house and pulled to a stop a hundred yards away in front of the cottage that stood under the oak grove. The cottage had been his grandmother's home in her later years, and was used infrequently as a guesthouse now. No one was supposed to be there.

Jogging down the front steps, he strode across the lawn, watching as a woman and a young boy emerged from the sedan. She walked confidently onto the porch and unlocked the front door. He had no idea what was going on, but he wasn't about to let it continue.

"Hey!"

The woman let the boy enter the cottage but didn't respond to his call. He quickened his steps. "Hey. What are you doing?" He reached the steps before she could disappear inside. "This is private property."

She turned to face him and he felt a stunned moment of awareness. Her emerald-green eyes were bright and inquisitive. Her strawberry blonde hair was held back on the sides with barrettes, allowing the wavy strands to tumble down behind her shoulders. He yanked his thoughts back into place. "You have no right to be here. So I suggest you hand me the key and leave." The green eyes darkened and she raised her chin, a slight smile touching her lips.

"Hello, Mr. Linc. As a matter of fact, I do have a right to be here. I'm your new tenant. My son and I will be staying in the cottage for the next few months."

Linc narrowed his eyes, sorting through the information. Only employees of his family's electrical contracting business called him Mr. Linc. It saved confusion between all the Montgomerys who worked there. His dad, Dale, himself and his two brothers, Seth and Gil. But he didn't recognize this woman, and she wasn't the type he'd forget.

"I don't know anything about that. No one told me.

Do you have a lease you can show me? Because if you don't, you'll need to leave. And if you refuse I'll have the sheriff out here to escort you off the property."

The boy he'd seen earlier rejoined the woman, whom Linc assumed was his mother. Standing close to her side and eyeing him with a hint of fear in his hazel eyes.

"Mom?"

"It's all right, Evan. This is Mr. Linc. His family owns the cottage. We're just discussing some of the details. You go back inside. I'll be there in a moment."

The boy nodded, then smiled up at his mother. "Mom, there's a river behind the house and tons of good climbing trees."

Linc spoke without thinking. "It's a creek. The Sandy Fork Creek."

The woman and boy stared at him with puzzled expressions. He was just trying to be correct.

The woman nudged the boy back inside, then came toward him, stopping at the edge of the top step and waiting. She raised her eyebrows. "If you'll allow me, I'll get the lease from my car and put your mind at ease."

For a reason he wasn't sure of, he refused to move. He wanted to challenge her. She was up to something, and he wasn't about to make it easy for her. He'd mastered the icy glare, the one that would send workers scattering back to their jobs, and difficult builders to bend to his will. He crossed his arms over his chest. "You do that."

She smiled as if dealing with a naughty child, then stepped deftly around him along the edge of the steps, brushing up against his arm and releasing a flowery scent that reminded him of the Confederate jasmine that grew along the side of the main house. He held his ground. Waiting. He kept his back to her, intending to show her who was in charge.

"Here you are. All signed and notarized."

She spoke from behind him, forcing him to turn and face her. He felt a flicker of admiration for her gutsy determination. Slowly he pivoted. She held out the paper and he took it with a quick swipe. He scanned the document twice to make sure he understood what he was reading. His mom had rented the cottage to this woman—a Gemma Butler—for free. Why? The lease was in order. His mother was the local real estate broker and she knew her stuff.

The woman held her hands clasped in front of her, her expression calm and a bit superior, elevating his blood pressure. He didn't like being made to look foolish. "Why is my mother letting you stay here free of charge?"

The woman lifted the lease from his hand with thumb and forefinger, then folded it and slipped it into her shoulder bag. "Perhaps you should ask her." She moved past him and up onto the porch. "Now, if you'll excuse me, I need to get my son settled. I have to start work in the morning. Have a nice day, Mr. Linc."

Linc watched the woman disappear inside the house and shut the door with a quiet snap. He dragged his fingers across his jaw. Great. This was the perfect ending to a lousy week. He'd been in Biloxi the past six days overseeing a mishandled construction project. When he'd returned home he'd found his mother gone to Little Rock to visit her sister. Now she'd taken on a tenant and had told him nothing about it.

He understood his mother was hurting and confused. Losing their father so suddenly to an aneurism had rocked their world. But she should have stayed here at home where she could be taken care of.

With his father gone, Linc was not only the head of the family now, but the head of Montgomery Electrical

Contractors, as well. The job should have been shared with his brother Gil, but he had left shortly after the funeral for Mobile to oversee a project there and to deal with an urgent personal matter. The responsibility of the company weighed heavily on Linc. He'd never realized how much he'd relied on his dad for advice and direction.

Jogging up the steps at the main house, Linc pushed through the front door and headed to the office at the far side of the large home. Pulling his cell phone from his pocket he dialed his mother, pacing the room as he waited. He was worried about her. It wasn't like her to run off to visit relatives without telling anyone, and it certainly wasn't like her to rent the cottage to someone outside the family. He'd lived in it himself for a while before getting his own place.

He barely let his mother say hello before he launched his barrage of questions. "You want to tell me about this woman in the cottage? Who is she and what's going on?"

"Hello, dear. Oh, she's there already. Good. Did you help her get settled in?"

Linc pressed his lips together to keep from saying something disrespectful. "No, ma'am, because I had no idea that we had a tenant. It would have been nice to have some warning, Mom."

"I'm sorry, dear. I meant to tell you, but I was in a hurry to get up here to see Mary and I guess I forgot."

"Who is she?"

"Gemma Butler."

"I saw that on the lease. Who *is* she?"

"From our accounting office. She needed to be closer to Dover when she starts work so I offered her the cottage."

Linc sank into the chair behind the desk, frustration

tightening his chest. "Mom. You're not making any sense. What work?" Silence. "Mom?"

"Well, honey. I should have told you, but I was—"

"In a hurry to get away. I got that." Why was she so anxious to leave the home she'd shared with his father? She should be here, working through her grief, not running off to her sisters.

"I resigned from the Christmas Event Committee. I just can't face it this year. So I recommended Gemma, and the Chamber of Commerce hired her. She's going to be wonderful."

He leaned forward, resting his elbows on the desktop. Trying to grasp the changes. "Mom, you've always done the Christmas events."

"I know, but not this year. Surely you understand. With your father gone…"

"I know." Nothing was the same with Dad gone. The world had tilted and they were all just trying to keep their balance. "When are you coming home?"

"I don't know. Next weekend, maybe. Have you talked to Gil?"

"No. Have you?"

"Yes. His attorney is still digging through legal tangles, but he's hopeful. The court should rule in his favor since he's the legal parent."

"Let's hope so. We both know the court system can often make poor decisions. I'm praying they won't this time."

Linc heard his mom hum her agreement, then encouraged her once more to come home before ending the call and tossing the cell onto the desk. His gaze landed on the family photo sitting on one corner. A short while ago they were all together. Now they were missing their most important member. Losing his dad had made him realize how much he valued his family, how important it was to stay close and keep the ties strong.

Unfortunately, the opposite was happening. His siblings seemed to be drifting away and he didn't know how to stop it. His sister Bethany had already left the fold years ago to pursue her dancing career in New York. Gil had moved to Mobile temporarily. Now his mother had quit her job and fled to her sisters. Seth was still here and so was his youngest sister, Victoria, but they'd been grieving, too, and he had no idea how to help them. He had no idea how to help himself. But his dad would have.

Pushing back from the desk, he stood and went to the window. He had a perfect view of the cottage, but saw no sign of the woman or boy. He searched his mind for a memory of her, but he couldn't recall ever seeing her in the office. He'd look her up on the employee files— better safe than sorry.

Turning from the window, he thought about her gutsy behavior. She'd stood up to him. Most women smiled and flirted. There was something different about Mrs. Butler. She looked all soft and feminine in her white lacy top and simple tan slacks. But underneath she was strong. Which was surprising since she wasn't very tall. Five-four tops. He stood an even six feet and she'd barely reached his shoulder.

He huffed out a breath and rubbed his forehead. He didn't need any more surprises. He had enough to deal with his father's passing and fighting to stay on top of things. He went to the window again, irritated to realize he was wondering where the woman was.

Gemma peeked out the master bedroom window of the small two-bedroom cottage at the stately mansion across the lawn. Linc Montgomery had disappeared inside several minutes ago, but her heart was only now settling into a normal rhythm. She'd watched him march across the grass, all broad shoulders and strong legs, unable to take her eyes off him. The man was positively imposing. Not to mention overbearing and arrogant. But she had to admit that despite his cold and egotistical demeanor, the Lord had blessed him with a physique that was hard not to admire.

He'd been blessed in the good-looks department, too. With his dark chocolate hair, deep blue eyes framed by thick lashes and a sharply defined jaw—he was definitely easy on the eyes. Too bad he was so obnoxious.

She'd only worked as an accountant for Montgomery Electrical for five months. She didn't necessarily enjoy her work, but the atmosphere had made up for it. The owner, Dale Montgomery, had made everyone feel valued and important. He knew each person's name, knew their children and spouses and never failed to offer prayer for those in need. She'd admired and respected him a great deal. His passing had left all the employees bereft.

When Mr. Linc and Mr. Gil had taken over, things had changed. She understood they were grieving, but she couldn't see herself working for Mr. Linc. Ever. He strode through the offices as if he was always on his way to someplace more important, only granting a nod to those he passed. He never smiled or offered a word of conversation. She'd been a bit surprised Linc hadn't recognized her, but she probably shouldn't be. She doubted he noticed anyone but himself.

It would have been nicer if Mr. Gil had been here when she arrived. He would have at least given her a pleasant welcome. Mr. Seth, too, would have been nice. He worked with the electricians and rarely came into the office, but the few times he had he'd been warm and friendly like his father. She knew nothing of the two sisters other than the tidbits she'd picked up from coworkers.

Francie was the one she truly adored. The matriarch of the Montgomery family was sweet, kind and generous. People were drawn to her warm personality and her caring heart. She owed the woman for freeing her from the accounting job and giving her a fresh start, and Gemma was determined to do a good job. She only wished Francie was here to talk to. She needed a little encouragement to meet with the president of the Dover Chamber of Commerce tomorrow.

Taking over as director of Christmas events was a big job and the Chamber was expecting her to create holiday attractions that would draw visitors and increase revenue. She clasped her hands beneath her chin and smiled. This was her second chance to make good.

Losing her event-planning business in Charlotte, North Carolina, last year had been devastating. Made more painful by the knowledge that her trusted friend and business partner, Darren Scofield, had betrayed her by stealing away her clients, then opening his own event business and leaving her with a worthless company. The fallout had been brutal. She'd been forced to return to her parents' home while she regrouped. A decision she deeply regretted. Her son had paid a high price for her mistake.

Evan peeked into her room. "Mom, can I go look at the river…I mean, the creek?"

"Not right now, sweetie. I have to finish unpacking, and I want to go with you to check it out. Are you all settled into your room?"

He nodded, the light in his hazel eyes revealing his excitement. "I can see the creek from my bed. This will be a cool place to explore."

She had to agree. Large trees, a stream and plenty of

room to run—it was an eight-year-old boy's dream. She knew Evan missed the generous backyard they'd had in Charlotte before her business had failed. She shook off the bad memories of those months. That was in the past. The Lord had answered her prayers and given her a new job and a new hope for her future. She gave her son a hug. "I think we'll both like it here."

The cottage was small and cozy, filled with lovingly worn upholstered furniture in the living room and charmingly mismatched tables and lamps. A fireplace added extra appeal. The dining and kitchen area flowed into each other and the multipaned window on the back wall looked out onto the shaded yard and the gnarled old oaks. But the best feature was the front porch that wrapped around one side of the cottage. She was looking forward to relaxing in one of the two wooden rockers. She hitched her shoulders and bit her lip. It was so nice to have a place of her own again.

The first notes of Kelly Clarkson's "Stronger" blasted from her cell phone. It had become her personal anthem during the past year. She smiled when she saw it was Caroline. After leaving her parents, she'd moved in with her college friend Caroline Walker in Sawyer's Bend, the next town over from Dover, and taken the job at Montgomery. "I figured I'd hear from you about now."

Her friend chuckled. "I just wanted to see how the big move was going. Do you think you'll like it there?"

Gemma smiled as she walked into the cheery blue-and-yellow kitchen. "The cottage is precious and Evan loves the yard, but I'm not so keen on the landlord."

"What do you mean? Francie is a sweetheart."

Caroline had worked several years for Montgomery Electrical until her jewelry design business had taken off. Now she ran a successful boutique in Sawyer's Bend. "I know, but that's not who greeted us. Mr. Linc did, and apparently he knew nothing about me renting the place."

"Oh, dear. Of all the brothers to get crossways of he would be the worst. Are you going to be okay there? With him around, I mean?"

"Of course. I don't like him much, but I'm not about to let him intimidate me. Besides, I have Francie on my side. I just wish she was here. This would be so much easier if she were."

"You can handle it. You're stronger than you think you are. And once you start planning all those Christmas events you'll be in your element again, and on your way back to the life you deserve. I'll come by soon to visit. I always wanted to get a close-up view of the mansion."

"Why not this afternoon? All I have to do is unpack a few clothes." The lack of response from her friend made her frown. "Caroline?"

"I'm meeting Vince this afternoon. I'm breaking it off."

"Why? I thought he was your perfect match."

"More like perfect mistake. I'll tell you about it later. But, Gemma, you're going to be spectacular at this Christmas thing. Gotta run."

Gemma ended the call with mixed emotions. Caroline was tossing aside another relationship without any real reason. But her support and encouragement renewed Gemma's confidence. Her friend was right. Planning events was her calling and her passion. She loved creating beautiful celebrations for her clients, giving them cherished memories of a special occasion.

Gemma peeked into the small bedroom and found Evan sitting cross-legged on the floor with his game player. She'd rather see him enjoying the outdoors. Maybe unpacking could wait. "Are you ready to go check out that creek?"

His eyes lit up, causing a prick in her heart. He'd lost his spark living with her parents. Staying with Caroline had helped ease some of his insecurities, but now that they were alone maybe he'd regain his happy smile and be less fearful and hesitant.

Fall leaves and small acorns crunched pleasingly beneath their feet as they crossed the yard on the way to the creek. It was a lovely piece of property with a lovely home to match. The pale-gray-and-white mansion rose three stories between hundred-year-old live oaks, thickly draped with Spanish moss. A circular porch with a balcony above graced one side of the home and a sunroom extended from the other side. Behind the house were two larger buildings she suspected had served as barn and stable in earlier times.

The overall effect was pleasing and welcoming. A true family home. The kind Gemma had always imagined.

"Mom, that guy, he was pretty strong, huh?"

"You mean Mr. Linc? Yes, I suppose he is." There was little doubt the man worked out.

"He looks like a quarterback. Suppose he played football?"

She didn't know for certain, but it was a safe assumption. He had the build for it and the aggressive personality. "Maybe." What had prompted her son's questions? Was he longing for a father figure in his life, someone to play ball and roughhouse with? Maybe she should have gotten married and given her son a real family. But she hadn't been able to bring herself to trust another man. She'd been betrayed too many times.

"Do I have to go to school tomorrow?"

She smiled at the dread in his voice. "Yes. We'll get

you registered first thing. I'm sure you'll make wonderful new friends."

He lowered his head and shrugged, kicking fallen leaves up as he walked. "I guess."

Gemma pulled him close for a quick hug. "Don't be afraid to talk to the other kids. I know it's been difficult for you staying with Grandma and Grandpa, then moving across the country to Miss Caroline's, but now it's just you and me, okay?"

"What if I make a mistake or do something wrong?"

Gemma set her jaw. Her perfectionist mother had chipped away at Evan's confidence with her constant criticism. Gemma had been so busy dealing with the aftermath from Darren's betrayal and losing her business she hadn't realized how hard it was for her son until the damage had been done. Growing up she'd grown a coat of armor against her mother's ways, but Evan was too young. When Caroline offered her a place, Gemma had jumped at the chance to escape the oppressive expectations of her overachieving parents.

"It's okay to make a mistake, Evan. And nothing on this earth is perfect, no matter what your grandmother says. You do the best you can and I'll always be proud of you. Understand?" Evan nodded and gave her a sweet smile.

They stopped at the edge of the creek. Broad and shallow, it posed little for her to worry about. Evan would have fun exploring. As he started to poke around the stones and mud, she wandered off a short ways. Her gaze drifted to the mansion. She stopped when movement caught her attention. A man stood at the edge of the porch. Linc. Was he watching them? Making sure they didn't do any damage? Had he talked to his mother?

She shook off the concerns. She had every right to be

here. If he didn't like it, that was his problem. Hers was creating a series of Christmas events that would give Dover the economic boost they needed. She already had lots of ideas and couldn't wait to meet with the Chamber members tomorrow to get started.

Unable to stop herself, she glanced at Linc again. Even across the distance his personality reached out and touched her—sending a shiver along her spine. She'd have to be vigilant. Strong. Keep her confidence in place. No one was going to make her cower, or take advantage of her ever again.

Chapter Two

Linc was not a fan of Monday mornings. Especially when it meant sitting behind a desk in an office. He'd much rather be in his truck headed for a job site. The figures on the page before him dissolved into a cloudy blur. He closed his eyes, rubbing them with his fingers to ease the strain. Calculating the estimates for a project bid was his brother Gil's area of expertise. Linc was more at home with managing the actual job. But with Gil in Mobile and Dad gone, it fell to him.

Leaning back in the chair, he scanned the office. His dad's presence lingered heavily in the air. At any moment he expected to hear his deep voice, and to see his sturdy frame striding into the room. The ache inside Linc's chest expanded, and a lump rose in his throat, so painful that it made his eyes burn.

As long as he could remember he'd wanted to be exactly like his dad. He wanted to do everything he did, including running the family business. But his dream had always included working side by side with his father— never running the company all alone. Technically, Gil was a partner, too. He was the planner, the negotiator, the one who won bids with his precise numbers. Linc was the hands-on guy, supervising the electricians, managing job sites and dealing with the construction issues.

He swiveled the chair to look out the window and studied the sign out front that proclaimed in shiny steel letters on a blue background the company his grandfather had started. Linc had trained and studied his whole life to assume this job. But he'd never expected the pressure involved with keeping a large company running.

He slammed a fist against the chair arm. Why had the Lord taken Dale Montgomery so young? He'd not seen his sixtieth birthday. His family needed him. Linc needed him. Setting his jaw, he shoved the self-pity aside and spun back around to the desk. He needed to buck up. His dad wouldn't want him behaving like a kid. He'd expect him to step in and take charge. Somehow Linc had to keep the company going and the family together. Family had meant everything to Dale Montgomery. Faith first, family second—then work.

"Hey, bro." Seth Montgomery strolled into the office and stopped in front of the desk. "I came by to pick up supplies and thought I'd see how you were doing."

Much of Linc's melancholy eased. His younger brother was easygoing and always found the bright side in everything. Linc rested his elbows on the desk. "Wishing Gil was here to figure out these blueprints. This bid is due at the end of the week."

Seth sat down with a shake of his head. "Don't look at me. I'm not the business type, remember? I like pulling wires and connecting circuit breakers." He grew serious as he glanced around the office. "It seems weird to see you in here instead of Dad."

The pressure inside Linc's chest squeezed like a vise, making it hard to breathe. They were all suffering the loss. "Trust me, it feels even weirder to sit here and try to do his job."

"Afraid you're not up to it?"

"Maybe."

Seth stood, an encouraging smile on his face. "Don't sweat it. You're the smartest guy I know. And the most stubborn. It might be rough at first, but you'll make it work. You and Gil together are a force, man."

"Thanks. Have you talked to Tori?" Their youngest sister had taken their father's death the hardest. As the baby of the family, she and Dad had shared a special bond. She was struggling with her grief.

"Yeah, she's not doing too well. She won't even let me come over. I'm worried. I wish Mom was here. Mom's the only one who can understand her."

"Hopefully she'll be home soon. Did you know she rented the cottage?"

"No. Who to?"

"A former employee of ours. Gemma Butler and her son."

Seth's serious expression shifted to one of appreciation. "Whoa. The pretty blonde from accounting?"

How did Seth know about her and he didn't? "Yeah. You know her?"

"Not really, but I had a payroll issue with one of the guys a while back and she got it all straightened out. Nice lady. Very sweet. And very single."

Linc had discovered that when he'd checked her file. "She's the new director of Christmas events for the Chamber."

"Really? Mom stepped aside, huh? I knew she was thinking about it."

Linc suddenly felt like a distant cousin instead of the eldest son. Everyone knew what was going on but him.

How had he missed all this? Maybe in his shock and grief he'd failed to pay attention. He'd have to do better. It was up to him now to stay involved in his siblings' lives. And his mother's. What else hadn't she told him? How was he supposed to be the head of the family if everyone kept him in the dark? Seth turned to leave. "Where are you working today?"

"Up in Madison. The Kramer house is behind schedule."

What else was new?

The rest of the day produced more annoyances and setbacks. By the time he called it quits, Linc was tired and ready to crash. After a quick shower and a sandwich, he refilled his glass of sweet tea and went out on the front porch. The air was rich with the smell of fall and the late-blooming camellias and roses. His gaze went immediately to the cottage. The silver car was parked along the narrow drive beside the house. There was no sign of the boy. He'd spotted him earlier in the yard tossing a football in the air. He'd considered offering to throw a few spirals to the kid, but then decided against it. Linc didn't need to get involved with the new tenants. Still, he found himself looking for her—Gemma. Unusual name but appropriate. With her red-gold hair and clear green eyes, she made him think of sparkling gemstones, like vibrant emeralds and fiery topaz. She was all soft and feminine, which made it all the more intriguing that she'd challenged him. She seemed too delicate to have such a strong backbone.

As he watched, the front door of the cottage opened and the object of his thoughts stepped onto the porch, settling into one of the rockers. With one leg folded under her, she pushed the rocker with her toe. She looked relaxed, dreamy, and he wondered what she was thinking. Part of him wanted to go talk to her. But a bigger part warned him to steer clear. The last thing he needed right now was any romantic distractions. Especially with a friend of his mother's. He pivoted and headed for the family room.

Monday Night Football was about to start.

The October twilight was pleasantly warm. A gentle breeze rustled the leaves on the ground in front of the cottage as Gemma kept the wooden rocker in motion. The light was fading, but she wasn't in any hurry to go inside as long as there was a single ray of light left to enjoy. Resting her head against the back of the chair, she closed her eyes, letting her senses appreciate the scents of autumn. She loved the mixture of earth, dry leaves and fading vegetation.

A sliver of guilt poked into her reverie. She'd come outside to read through the folder that Pete McCorkle, president of the Dover Chamber of Commerce, had given her on the town's previous celebrations—not to daydream.

A busy squirrel screeched from a nearby tree, making the hair on the back of her neck tingle. No. It wasn't the critter that had her senses on alert. She opened her eyes. Someone was watching her. She glanced toward the main house, expecting to find Linc looking at her again. But the porch was empty. She looked at the large window on the side of the house. Was he watching from that room? She fought the urge to retreat inside.

The sensation faded, and she relaxed. She must be imagining things. Linc's scrutiny earlier had left her edgy. But she refused to worry about his bad attitude or his effect on her nervous system. In her line of work she'd learned how to deal with all types of people, from the overly friendly to the overly hostile. But Linc triggered emotions that were unfamiliar and disturbing. Until she could put a name to them, she was keeping her guard up and plenty of distance between herself and the eldest Montgomery brother. Linc was exactly the type she wanted to avoid. Overly confident, arrogant and with a need to take charge.

Opening the folder in her lap, she leafed through the reports Pete had given her. There wasn't much to look at. They consisted of a small parade, random lights around town, a nativity, a Christmas tree in the square park and a lighted star on the courthouse dome.

They'd given Gemma to the end of the week to come up with ideas to transform their ho-hum celebration into something spectacular that would be a draw for holiday tourists, and in turn boost their sagging economy. Most of her responsibility would fall on the first two weekends of the celebration. She wouldn't be involved with the other two events, the community meal for the needy and the toy drive, but she already had ideas for a few additions that would hopefully enhance them.

Her creative juices were already flowing. She'd come up with a dozen ideas, and with the budget she'd been given she shouldn't have any trouble seeing them through. She and Evan had made a tour of downtown yesterday and explored some of the neighborhoods. If she could get enough of the business owners on the square motivated, she could make Christmas in Dover an event people flocked to each year. She could see it growing steadily and someday being named in the top ten attractions in the South. Maybe even a feature article in *Southern Living* magazine.

She chuckled softly. She was getting ahead of herself. First she had to get her ideas approved.

"Hey, Mom. What'cha doing?"

Gemma smiled as her son joined her on the porch. "Looking over some work for tomorrow. Did you run out of time on your video game?" She'd set strict limits on the amount of time Evan could spend on his games.

"Yes, ma'am. Can I play under those trees until dark?"

"Sure."

Refocusing on the file, her confidence wavered. She had a lot to accomplish between now and December 1. Thankfully the Chamber heads were eager for her to succeed. And she *needed* to succeed. Failure meant accepting help from her parents. She'd imposed on Caroline long enough, and moving back home would be emotional suicide. But with a mountain of debt, working as a low-level accountant would barely provide a living for her and Evan.

Gemma ran her hands through her hair, staring up at the passing clouds. As long as she could remember her parents had pressured her and her older sister, Beatrice, to achieve greatness. Nothing less would do. Her father, a well-known professor of political science, and her mother, head of a large private foundation, had expected even more from their daughters. Bea had done her part by earning her doctorate.

Gemma was the black sheep. Her creative bent had been a puzzlement to her parents, something they didn't understand or condone. To them it was a waste of time to draw or paint. She'd fought them her whole life, even down to taking piano lessons. If she wasn't going to be a concert pianist, what was the point?

She'd compromised by getting a second degree in accounting, but she had no intension of getting her CPA— an achievement her parents ceaselessly pressured her to attain. Accounting was a handy skill to have to fall back on, but event planning was her passion.

Determined to prove herself and carve out her own life, she'd started Fine Day Events with her good friend Darren. Their business had been a huge success, fulfilling all of Gemma's hopes. Until Darren had betrayed her and destroyed her dream.

But she'd learned her lesson. This time she would rely only on her own skills and abilities. She was an exceptional event planner, and she would turn Dover's holiday celebrations into something everyone in south Mississippi would flock to see.

Nothing would stand in her way.

Linc's cell phone rang the moment he changed the channel to ESPN and settled back for a distracting game on *Monday Night Football*. He groaned and picked up his phone. Mom. Maybe she was coming home. Finally. "Mom. How's it going?"

"Fine. I was just calling to ask you if you'd made our new tenant comfortable. I want her to feel welcomed so I hope you're going by and checking on her."

"I'm not the welcoming committee, Mom. I'm sure if she needs anything she'll ask."

"Does she have your number?"

"I don't know."

"John Lincoln, you make yourself available to that young woman. She's taking on a big job and we need to be there for her."

"Mom, I have my hands full trying to run the business. I don't have time to play host."

"Do you know if she's met with the Chamber folks yet?"

Linc rubbed his forehead. "No. I've only spoken to her once."

"Son, I've dumped a big project in her lap and I'm

not there to guide her. I want you to attend those meetings and make sure she has all she needs. You've helped me with Christmas events several times and you know what to do."

"Mom, maybe it's time you came home. We miss you. Especially now. Tori's not doing well. If you were here you could help this woman yourself. It would keep you busy and your mind off…things."

"You think keeping busy will make me forget I lost the man I've loved for nearly forty years?"

His mother's harsh tone humbled him. "You know that's not what I meant."

"I'll be home soon. I promise. And I've been talking to your sister. She just needs to work through this in her own way. In the meantime, you watch over Gemma. She's a good friend and I want her to know we're supporting her."

"Friend? Mom, how do you know this woman?"

"Remember the retirement party for Harvey Morgan? She's the one who planned that whole thing. It was amazing. I went to tell her what a splendid job she'd done and we connected right away. I think she's exactly what Dover needs to spark up the Christmas events."

What was going on? "The events are just fine the way they are."

"Be that as it may, will you do as I ask and look out for her?"

"Fine. I'll pay her a visit tonight."

"Thank you, dear. I love you."

"Love you, too, Mom."

Linc hung up, then lay his head on the back of the recliner. So much for the football game. He needed downtime, a few hours of mindless distraction from the pressure at the office. The last thing he wanted to do was play gracious host to the new tenant. In fact, he'd like to avoid the woman altogether. Something about her disturbed him, but he wasn't sure what or why. He'd even dreamed about her last night. Not a good thing.

He didn't understand why his mother was so concerned about the woman handling the job. Mom had the decorations and celebrations down to a science. All that Gemma had to do was follow the plan from the previous years and it would be a breeze. But, as he'd promised his mom, first he'd make her feel welcomed.

Leveraging himself from the recliner, he went to the freezer in the utility room and pulled out one of his mom's frozen pecan pies. Her standard welcome-to-the-area offering.

Slipping on his athletic shoes, he didn't bother to tie the laces. This would be a quick howdy-do. He'd hand her the pie, offer her his assistance, then get back to the game. The Saints had the ball.

All the lights in the cottage were blazing when he knocked on the door. He shifted impatiently as he waited. He'd reached out to knock again when the door opened and Gemma appeared. The lights from inside framed her in a soft glow, making her skin translucent and her reddish-blond hair spark with light. She was stunning. His mouth went dry and he forgot why he was here. "Uh. My mom, I mean, I brought you a pie. Pecan pie." He went warm all over. What was wrong with him? He never had trouble talking to women, but for some reason he was as tongue-tied and awkward as a teenager with his first crush. "I should have brought it sooner. To welcome you. As a tenant." He suddenly wished the porch boards would collapse and swallow him into the ground.

She smiled, her green eyes twinkling like emeralds.

"That's very kind of you. I'm sure Francie would have brought it herself if she was here."

Linc frowned. Was she implying that he obviously hadn't thought of this himself? She was right, but he didn't like the idea that she could read him. "Actually, I wanted to bring it as an apology gift, too." Good move. Now he was back on track. "I wasn't very hospitable yesterday when you arrived. I didn't know Mom had leased the cottage. And, uh, I've been too busy to get over here before this."

She raised an eyebrow, then dropped her gaze down to his feet and his untied laces. "And you were so anxious to get the pie to me that you forgot to tie your shoes?"

"No. I—" Heat infused his neck and cheeks. Linc Montgomery didn't like being off balance. He was always the one in charge. This woman was downright irritating.

"My son does that when he's in a hurry to finish an unpleasant task. Like taking out the garbage, or bringing a pie to a neighbor."

Her eyes weren't twinkling now. They were dark and challenging. Well, he'd show her. He flashed his best smile. "A neighbor I should get to know better. Where would you like me to put this?" He stepped closer, edging past her to the door. She was not going to get the best of him.

She moved aside, following him into the living room. "Just put it in the kitchen."

He smiled over his shoulder. "It's frozen."

"So you didn't bake it yourself, then?"

"I could have." He cringed at the stupidity of that remark. He could no more bake a pie than knit a sweater. Mr. Smooth Moves with the ladies was playing one-upmanship with a girl. No, a woman. A disturbingly attractive and quick-witted one at that.

She stood in the small eating area while he placed the pie on the counter. He looked at her and smiled again. She didn't smile back. "So is there anything I can do for you? Anything need fixing, problems with the house, something up high I can get down for you?"

She arched her brows. "Everything is fine. We don't need a thing. And I have a step stool."

"Hey, Mom." The boy charged into the room, his shoes squeaking on the floor when he stopped. "Hi, Mr. Linc."

Linc searched his memory for the boy's name. "Hey, Evan." He noticed the junior-size football in the boy's hands. "You play?"

"Naw. Mom can't throw and I don't know anyone yet."

"I'll play with you. Just holler. When you see that red truck at the main house that means I'm home. I love football."

The boy's face split in a wide smile. "Did you play?"

"Sure did. All through college."

"Pro, too?"

"No. I wasn't tall enough." He shrugged. "Only six feet."

"Drew Brees is only that tall."

"Yes, but *he* has talent."

Evan chuckled, then hurried from the room.

Gemma gave him a cool glare. "That was very nice of you. Assuming you follow up on your offer?"

"Why wouldn't I?"

She shrugged. "I've learned people say a lot of things they don't mean. Promises aren't worth much."

"They are to me."

"That remains to be seen, doesn't it?"

He'd had enough. This woman was getting under his skin. She shoved him off balance every time she spoke, and with every glance from those incredible green eyes.

Seeing a pen and notepad on the counter, he scribbled down his cell number. "If you need anything, call. Day or night. I mean that."

"Of course you do. Your mother would tan your hide if you didn't. Right?"

Either she didn't think much of him or she knew his mother better than he'd expected. Whatever—he wasn't going to expend any more effort on making her feel at home. His mom could do that when she got back. "Good night." He walked past the table and noticed the photos from last year's Christmas events. Beside them were sketches of the same scenes, only far more elaborate. He touched one sketch with his fingertips. "What are these?"

Gemma came to his side. "My designs for decorating the downtown."

"But this looks nothing like it did last year."

"That's the point. The Chamber wants to expand everything. More lights, more activities, more decorations."

"Why?"

"To bring in more business. Over the next few years they'd like to see Dover become a Christmas destination spot."

"Does my mother know about this?"

"Yes. Of course."

Blindsided again. Linc nodded and made his way to the door. Everything in his life was upside down and backward. Gemma followed him.

"Thank you for the pie."

He stopped and looked back at her, caught again by how lovely she was. "You're welcome."

Linc made his way down the steps, nearly tripping on his laces. He propped his foot up on a planter and tied them before marching back to the house.

This Gemma was going to completely change Dover's

Christmas. He liked it the way it was. Time to have another talk with his mother. Surely she didn't intend for this woman to toss out the cherished holiday celebrations.

Suddenly his mom's suggestion that he attend the Chamber meetings and help Gemma sounded like a great idea. His mom was right about one thing. He did know the Christmas events down to the last plastic poinsettia. He'd make sure she didn't destroy the holiday traditions the people in this town treasured—and that she kept things the way his mother always had.

Gemma closed the door behind Linc, then returned to the kitchen and stared at the pie. That *had* to have been Francie's idea. She seriously doubted Linc would think of that on his own.

She smiled as she imagined Linc's reaction to Francie's request to bring a pie to the new tenants. No doubt he'd whined and rolled his eyes the way Evan did when faced with an unpleasant task. Why else would Linc traipse over here with his shoes untied?

When she'd seen him coming up on the porch, she'd braced for another confrontation and assumed her most pleasant expression. The one she used for clients who were inclined to be difficult. But when she'd opened the door, he'd looked stunned—and confused. He'd recovered quickly, unleashing his charm, but it was obvious he was unhappy with playing gentleman host.

It was all a wasted effort where she was concerned. She felt certain he was accustomed to women melting under his disarming smile, and to be fair, it had caused a small hitch in her breath. She doubted he was used to women challenging his motives.

What he didn't know was how fragile her bravado actually was. Resting a hand on her throat, she took a few deep breaths to slow her heart rate and calm the flutters in her stomach.

She'd have to keep her head around Linc. He put the electric in Montgomery Electrical. Energetic and aggressive, with his piercing blue eyes, the perpetual scowl on his chiseled features, he was the kind of man who could overpower you with his personality alone. Which meant he wasn't the kind of man she ever intended to get close to. The thought of being overpowered again chilled her blood. She forced the memory back into the dark corner of her mind, praying for peace. The past was over. She had Evan. That was all she wanted to remember.

"Mom? Did that man leave?"

She motioned her son to her side. "Yes. Why?"

He exhaled a loud sigh. "I wanted to ask him about football and stuff."

Gemma's shoulders sagged at the thought. Another challenge to guard against. She didn't need her son developing a case of hero worship for a man like Linc. Though he had been kind to Evan earlier, she knew better than to make any snap judgments about men. Besides, Linc hadn't come of his own accord in a gesture of welcome or apology. He'd come because he'd been ordered by his mother.

"We'll talk about that tomorrow. It's time for bed."

After settling Evan for the night, Gemma returned to the dining room to go over her presentation one more time. She'd spent a good portion of the past two days sketching out ideas for decorating the town square. Looking at her drawings released a bubble of excitement from deep inside—helping to chase away the unease Linc had left in his wake. Tomorrow she would meet with the Chamber officials to present her preliminary plans, and she needed to be prepared. If she succeeded in Dover, it would open the doors for her future. She could return to Charlotte, or anywhere for that matter, and start another business. New name, new focus, new goals. Ones that didn't include trusting someone else.

Chapter Three

Gemma waited patiently the next afternoon as the officers of the Dover Chamber of Commerce passed around her drawings for the downtown Christmas decorations. She'd received a warm welcome from everyone. She'd already met Pete McCorkle, the president, but this afternoon she'd been introduced to Celia Jones, the membership director; Jeff Wilson, director of sales; and the treasurer, Leon Skelton. They had expressed their excitement over the expansion of the Christmas celebrations. She'd also met Leatha Delmar, who would be her assistant, and who had greeted her with a warm hug and assurance that she would help with everything. As a long-time resident of Dover, Leatha's knowledge and experience would be invaluable.

Pete studied her drawings, a pleased smile on his face. "These are wonderful. This should draw people from up in Jackson to come down and see our decorations." He glanced at her. "Can you do this within the budget?"

"I believe so. Provided we can get the business owners on board to help. I'm hoping for a few volunteers to help me coordinate details and work with store owners. And I'll solicit donations where I can. I'd like to incorporate the other events you have—the community dinner, the toy drive. Bring all the events together, which will ultimately help all the merchants, not just the ones around the square."

Celia nodded in agreement. "I don't think you'll have any trouble. For years, we've wanted to do more with Christmas beyond tossing up a few lights."

"May I ask why you haven't?"

"Money, mainly. We have two other large events and fund-raisers during the year. A Founders Day celebration in the fall, and a sidewalk sale and cook-off in the spring. It's only been with the closure of the Southways plant that we were forced to look for another means of revenue. We decided to make more of our charming downtown and put more effort into the holiday."

"I think that was a wise decision. Your town square is ideal for showcasing Christmas celebrations."

Pete clasped his hands on the table. "I like your ideas and your enthusiasm. How soon can we get started on this? I'm afraid we haven't given you much time. It's already late October."

Gemma kept her demeanor professional, but inside she wanted to leap for joy. "I'd like to start with a meeting of the local business owners as soon as possible. I'd also like to see what you have on hand as far as lights, signs, banners, holiday decor, things like that."

Jeff Wilson spoke up. "That would be in the storage building over on Fifth Street. Francie Montgomery should be able to give you her key."

Gemma bit her lip. "Oh. I'm afraid she's out of town, and I have no idea when she'll be home."

Wilson waved off her concern. "No problem—Linc will know where the key is."

She forced a smile, but inwardly she cringed. She was

trying to avoid Linc—not become more involved. The memory of his unexpected visit last night sent her pulse racing and released a swarm of butterflies in her stomach. Still, she left the meeting with a confidence she hadn't felt in a long time.

She smiled through her trip to the grocery, the bank and the drugstore. When she pulled up at the school to pick up Evan she was still smiling. Tomorrow she would take pictures of the downtown buildings so she could begin designing light displays. She'd draft an email to the business owners tonight requesting a meeting in the next couple of days. She prayed they would be willing to participate. But first she had to see what was salvageable in the storage building. Unfortunately, to do that she needed to talk to Linc again and get the key.

"Hey, Mom." Evan slid into the front seat and buckled up.

"How did it go today?" She reached over and smoothed his hair.

"Good. I met a boy who lives near us. He said if you'll call his mom she would let him come over to play."

"That's wonderful, honey. Did you get her number?"

"Yes, ma'am."

Gemma made the turn into the winding driveway of the Montgomery estate situated a few miles south of downtown Dover. The long alley of live oaks arching overhead, dripping with moss, was like a loving welcome home. Living on the Montgomery estate in the quaint cottage gave her a sense of belonging and fueled her imagination. Her mind was a tumbler of ideas all straining to spill forth and become reality.

As she made the curve to the main house she noticed Linc's red Silverado parked in front. She would have expected him to drive a black one. It better suited his personality. She didn't relish the idea of approaching him again. He'd probably want proof that she had permission to open the storage building.

She squared her shoulders and raised her chin. She was a professional. She'd ask for the key, then go on about her business. Piece of cake. Or in his case, pie.

"Mom, can I see if Mr. Linc can play football with me?"

"Honey, I'm sure he's working. He's a busy man. We shouldn't bother him."

"But he said he liked to play. He said I could ask him."

Gemma stole a quick glance at her son, a twinge of sadness settling in her chest. How could she explain to her son that people often made offhand promises they didn't really mean? She knew the heartbreak of trusting the wrong person. She didn't want her son to know that kind of betrayal. But she couldn't fill him with fear of others or of having friends and relationships, either. Sooner or later she knew he'd get his little heart broken and all she could do was be there to help him through it. But she'd make sure he knew that the Lord was always with him and that He was the only trustworthy presence.

Stopping beside the cottage, she switched off the engine and faced her son. "Change your clothes first, then you can go ask. But be polite and remember he might be too busy so don't be disappointed if he says no."

"Thanks, Mom."

He scurried out of the car and dashed up onto the porch, fidgeting impatiently while she unlocked the door.

Within minutes he was out the door, football cradled in his arm, and racing across the lawn to the main house. She debated whether to watch him from the porch or take a more discreet position from inside. She hoped Linc would say yes, but her common sense knew he'd probably turn the boy away, leaving her to deal with the fallout.

She should have gone with him. She had a perfect excuse—she needed the key to the storage building. But subjecting herself to his dynamic personality wasn't a good idea. Evan's father had been a forceful, compelling man. She shook off the painful memory and hurried to her bedroom window. Leaning against the frame, she swallowed a wave of shame. She'd let her own fears and insecurities stop her from accompanying her son. But she couldn't go with him everywhere.

She watched as Evan waited at the front door. Linc had better answer or she'd give the man a piece of her mind. He shouldn't make careless promises to little boys. The mansion door opened and she saw Evan look up. Her son nodded. Then nodded again more slowly and turned and headed down the porch steps.

Gemma pressed a hand over her mouth. Linc was sending the boy away. She braced herself for tears. Evan ran across the lawn, but stopped midway, tossing the ball in the air.

Puzzled, she leaned closer to the window and saw Linc jogging easily toward Evan. He raised his hands and Evan tossed the ball. It fell short. Linc scooped it up and motioned Evan to his side, then proceeded to demonstrate the correct way to hold and throw the ball.

Surprise drew Gemma's lips apart and warmth filled her chest. She'd been fully prepared for Linc to dismiss his invitation. He didn't strike her as the kind of guy who would want to spend time with a child. She watched as Evan tossed the ball and Linc made a big show of catching it. After one toss, Linc fell to the ground and Evan threw himself on top of him. The happy smile on her son's face tightened her throat and brought tears to her eyes. He needed this. A man to do guy things with. She'd tried to fill that void, but as a single mom it was all she could do to keep things on track. Lately, even that had been impossible.

She glanced out again and saw Linc staring at her. Her skin heated. Even across the distance and through the window, his piercing gaze caused a skip in her heartbeat. He motioned her to join them. Curious, she went out and across the lawn.

"Mom, Mr. Linc wants me to join his team. Can I?"

"Team? What kind of team?" Gemma looked at Linc for an explanation.

"I coach a kid's football team. It's through the church." He shrugged. "My brother Gil is actually the coach, but I took it over when he went to Mobile. We practice twice a week after school and our games are on Saturdays. The cost is reasonable. Basically for a shirt and registration fees."

His offer surprised her. "Football. I don't know, Evan. It's a rough sport." Her expression must have revealed her concern because Linc hastened to explain.

"It's flag football, Gemma. No helmets or pads, no tackling. They wear a belt with tear-away flags on each side. They pull the flags to tackle."

That sounded safe. "Well, I'll think about it."

Evan looked up at her with soulful eyes. "Please, Mom."

How could she refuse? This was what she'd hoped for when she'd moved here. But why did the offer have to involve Linc?

Linc ruffled Evan's hair. "Come to the house and I'll give you the registration packet to look over. It explains everything. And if you still have concerns you can come to the game this Saturday and see how it works."

His consideration surprised her. Being on a team would be good for Evan. It would help him make friends and boost his confidence. She'd been too busy running her own business to find the time to take him to ball practices. Something else he'd missed out on. Along with not having a dad. "All right." She started across the lawn. Evan hurried ahead, leaving her and Linc to walk together. "Thank you for playing with him."

"You didn't think I'd remember, did you?"

"No. I didn't."

One dark eyebrow arched. "So is it just me or do you not trust people in general?" Without waiting for an answer he pushed open the door and went inside.

Gemma stepped into the grand foyer, her interest immediately captivated by the beauty of the burled-wood panels on the walls and the broad staircase with its stained glass window on the landing. The scent of furniture polish and old wood lay thick in the air and was a testament to the loving care the home had received over the years. But what struck her most profoundly was the sense of warmth and welcome that embraced her.

Her parents' home was large, but sleek and formal. It had been featured in a design magazine once. But no one would ever call it homey or welcoming.

Linc appeared from a doorway on the left, holding a sheet of paper in his hand. "This should tell you everything you need to know. Unfortunately the season has already started so he won't get to play all the games listed here, but I think he'll enjoy it." He smiled at Evan. "The boy runs fast."

Evan beamed. "Can I play this weekend?"

Gemma swallowed the lump in her throat. It had been a long time since she'd seen him so happy, and she owed it to Linc's kindness. "I'll do my best."

Evan let out a whoop.

Linc grinned. "Just get me the paperwork and I'll make sure he plays. We can borrow a shirt if we have to."

Gemma squeezed her son's shoulder. "Then, we'd better get back home and start filling out forms."

"Thanks, Mr. Linc."

"You're welcome, buddy." The pair shared a high five.

"Hey, Mr. Linc, do you know a kid named Cody Fenelli?"

"I do. His family lives up the road. His dad and I went to college together. Why?"

"I want him to come and play. Is that okay? I mean, this being your house and all."

"Of course. I'll give them a call. He's on the team, too."

"Really? Oh, wow, this is so cool." Evan dashed out and back to the cottage.

Gemma walked to the door, searching for the right words to express her appreciation. "Thank you for this. He's had a rough time of things lately. Playing on a team with other boys is an answer to my prayers."

Linc set his hands on his hips, a half smile moving his lips. "I've never been an answer to a prayer before."

She pressed her lips together. Leave it to him to think the comment was personal. "Oh, I doubt that. I'm sure there are plenty of females who think you're God's gift."

"Is that a compliment?"

"No. I've known men like you. All charm on the outside, but inside no emotion and little substance. Thanks again." She walked across the porch, acutely aware of Linc coming behind her. The man made the air around him vibrate with energy. Being near him sent odd flutters through her stomach and made her nerves all quivery. She didn't like the sensation. Not one bit.

The key. She stopped and turned around. Linc plowed into her from behind. Her foot slipped off the porch edge, throwing her off balance.

"Whoa."

Strong arms grabbed her waist and set her on the porch. Breathless, she fought through the confusion and found herself pressed against Linc's chest, her hands resting over his heart, which was beating rapidly. She inhaled his woodsy aftershave deep into her lungs. She looked up into his eyes and saw concern etched in the blue depths.

She told herself to pull away. But her body refused to obey her mind's commands. She was too surprised. Not that she was in his arms—she could rationalize that—but what had her flummoxed was the realization that Linc Montgomery was warm and very human. She'd assumed being close to him would be similar to standing in front of an open refrigerator—cool and icy. Instead of wanting to pull away, she was oddly content to remain right where she was.

Horrified at the thought, she stepped back, putting a safe distance between herself and her landlord. "Sorry. I thought of something else I wanted to ask."

"You okay?"

"Yes. But I need the key to the Christmas storage building. They said you would know where it is?" She cleared her throat, disgusted at the shaky tremor in her voice.

Linc flashed a smile that filled his blue eyes with amusement. Arrogant man. Now he'd think he had some effect on her. Which was ridiculous. She was too smart, too battle scarred to ever let that happen again.

"I'll go look for it right now."

"Okay, that would be, uh…" She stared at the paper in her hands. "Great. I'll get it when I return the forms."

Gemma hurried down the steps, careful to not trip. Blood roared in her ears; every nerve in her body was on fire. Of all the dumb clichés. Tripping and having the big strong man catch her. Ugh. She didn't need a big strong guy. Least of all one who had an ego larger than the entire state of Mississippi.

Safely inside the cottage, Gemma sat at the table and began filling out the form. Gil Montgomery's name was listed as coach, and she wished he was still here to fill that role. Though she had to admit Linc had suggested the team to Evan and followed through by making sure they got the paperwork. And she couldn't forget how he'd brought the pie. He hadn't wanted to come, but he had because he honored his mother. A commandment she herself struggled with.

Linc was challenging her assumptions about him. She'd got a glimpse of the man behind the stony facade and it wasn't at all what she expected. Maybe he wasn't all bad. Just mostly.

Her conscience twitched as she remembered her words to him on the porch. *Little substance.* While she might believe that, she shouldn't have voiced her opinion. She'd meant her comments to be teasing, but some of her deep-seated bitterness had crept into her tone. Linc's eyes had filled with a flash of hurt and surprise. She'd obviously pricked his ego with her statement. She shouldn't waste too much time feeling remorse. He'd get over it.

What mattered now was getting this paperwork back to him so Evan could play ball this weekend. Her son was her life. She'd endure anything for his sake, including standing on the sidelines while Linc coached the team.

But for some reason she still felt bad about labeling him. Even if it were true.

Linc pivoted and strode back into the house, scolding himself for letting his tenant's words get to him. *Lit-*

tle substance. She obviously didn't think much of him. But what disturbed him more was the reaction she'd unleashed when he'd pulled her into his arms to keep her from falling down the brick steps.

She'd been warm and soft cradled against him. Her scent had disrupted his senses and sent his thoughts pinballing in a dozen different directions. She felt right in his arms and he'd wanted to hold her forever. She'd felt it, too. The awareness. He'd seen it in her eyes. But he also knew she'd deny it. Maybe he could change her opinion of him.

"Linc!"

He recognized the shout. His sister Victoria was here. He met her in the hall. "Hey, sis. Everything okay?"

She glanced around the room, tears welling in her eyes. "No. Nothing is okay. I miss him so much."

He wrapped an arm around her shoulder. "Is there anything I can do?" Here was his chance to step up and fill in for Dad.

"No. I came to tell you that I'm going away for a while."

Linc clenched his teeth and stepped away. Why was everyone leaving? "Tori, this is no time to be running away. We need to stick together. Mom will be home soon and she'll need you here. She needs *all* of us more than ever now."

His sister shook her head and brushed away tears. "I can't handle being around the house without Dad here. I'm going to visit my friend Judy in California. It'll give me time to sort things out."

"Why can't you do that here?"

Her eyes narrowed and she pressed her lips together. "I knew you'd say that. Why does it matter? Gil and Beth aren't here, either."

"Bethany is working, and Gil is fighting for custody of his daughter."

"And I'm fighting for my sanity." She shook her head, scowling. "I knew you wouldn't understand. You're not like the rest of us."

He planted his hands on his hips. "What's that supposed to mean?"

"You don't feel like we do. You're not emotional."

He winced. Gemma had said the same thing. Didn't they understand he felt just as deeply as anyone else? He simply chose not to expose his emotions for the world to see.

Tori reached out and touched his arm. "I'm sorry, Linc. I didn't mean that the way it sounded. I know you're hurting, too. See how upset I am? I need to get away."

"You mean run away. Like Mom."

"It's not running away, it's stepping aside and trying to deal with the grief." She slipped her arm around his waist. "It's too fresh here, Linc, too raw. I need to get some perspective. That's why Mom went to Aunt Mary's. It's too hard to sort through the pain when you're surrounded by memories."

"Some of us have to stay and deal with the realities."

"You're the big brother. You can handle anything." Tori patted his cheek. "I already told Mom. I'll keep in touch, promise."

"What about the real estate office? I thought you were running it while she's gone."

"Mom said to close it down. Business is slow. Besides, she'll be home in a few days."

Linc walked his sister to the front porch. He'd never felt as helpless, like a catfish floundering on a dock. The harder he tried to keep the family together the faster they seemed to pull away. It didn't make any sense.

Tori stopped on the porch and faced him. "I love you, big brother. We all depend on you. Now that Dad is… You're our rock." She wrapped him in a warm hug.

Did Tori have any idea the weight of that responsibility? "You'll be home for Thanksgiving, won't you?"

"I don't think I could celebrate without Dad here. It will be too awful." She glanced over his shoulder and smiled.

He looked around and saw Gemma standing at the edge of the sidewalk holding the registration forms. "Done already?"

"Evan is eager to be on the team."

"Gemma, this is my baby sister, Victoria. Tori, this is Gemma Butler, she's…"

"Taking over Mom's job. I know." She stepped forward and shook Gemma's hand. "Nice to meet you. Mom thinks you're very talented. I can't wait to see all the changes you'll make. It's about time we expanded our Christmas events. It's the happiest time of the year and we barely do anything."

"I'll do my best."

Linc started to protest, but Tori said goodbye and hurried to her car. Even Tori knew about the new tenant. Gemma handed the paperwork to Linc. "Your sister seems very nice."

"She's leaving. She can't handle being around memories of Dad." He hadn't meant to blurt that out.

"Oh. Were they close?"

"Very. She's the youngest so—" He shrugged. "You know how dads and their baby girls are."

"No, actually I don't."

Linc looked at her. There was an emptiness and a hint of sadness in her eyes. "You're not close to your father?"

"No. Is that all you need? I've attached a check."

Linc looked at the papers. "Yeah. That should do it."

"Fine. I'll get directions to the ball field later. Did you find the key?"

The businesslike tone of her voice said she was eager to be away from him. "No. I haven't had a chance to look. I didn't expect you back so soon. I'll let you know when I do."

"Good. I'd like to get started. I've got a lot to organize."

She walked away, leaving Linc with a lot of questions. What changes? The over-the-top stuff he'd seen in her drawings? What was wrong with their events the way they were now? And why was he always the last one to know anything lately? Even Tori, who'd been a virtual recluse these past weeks, had known about Gemma and their mother's plans to step down from the committee. He'd had enough. Time to get involved.

He walked back inside, another question dogging his heels. What was behind the cold tone in Gemma's voice when she mentioned family? And why did she never talk about the boy's father?

Gemma sorted through her papers and notes Wednesday afternoon as she waited for the town square business owners to start arriving at the courthouse conference room. Her nerves tingled with excitement as she worked. This was her joy, the thing that gave her satisfaction and fulfillment. She couldn't wait to get started.

Glancing at the door, her confidence sagged. What if no one showed up? What if the owners refused to participate in the celebrations? Closing her eyes, she offered up a quick prayer for patience and greater faith. The Lord had set her on this path, which meant He had a plan. She just needed to trust it would work out. Operative word— *trust*. Not an easy thing to do.

"Is this the Christmas meeting?"

Gemma smiled at the gentleman who entered the room, her doubts melting away like snowflakes. "Yes, it is."

Within the next few minutes a good portion of the forty store owners on the square filed in. She stepped to the lectern, encouraged at the turnout. With little time before the start of the holiday season, it would take everyone's involvement to pull off the four weekend events she had designed.

"Welcome. I'm Gemma Butler. I've spoken with some of you by phone and met a few of you. Thank you for being here this afternoon. I know meeting in the middle of the day is difficult for you, but we don't have much time to get these events organized. We'll meet again next Thursday evening. I'll have a more detailed plan drawn up at that time." Gemma smiled around the room. "Keep in mind the key ingredient is enthusiasm and determination. And of course a lot of elbow grease."

A man in the front row spoke up. "I don't mind the work, but I don't have the money to spend on lots of decorations."

"I understand that, and we do have a budget that will help you with some of the expenses. Mainly I want to work with each merchant to craft a unique holiday display that will reflect your business. Our goal is to draw people to Dover to learn about your shops, to expose them to the unique personality of the town and make them want to make future trips to Dover to spend their time and their money."

A woman raised her hand. "I'm an insurance agent.

Putting up a tree in my front window isn't likely to gain me any new clients. I'm reluctant to spend too much time on Christmas events that won't help my bottom line."

"That raises a good point. I'd like you to think of this on a larger scale than one business. It's true some of your businesses lend themselves to the holidays more than others—the dress shops and gift shops, for example. But if visitors see how your community works together for the good of all, think what kind of message that sends. That would make Dover a place I'd want to visit, perhaps even come to live, and that would benefit every business in town."

Agreeable murmurs traveled through the room. "I've heard about the way this town comes together. One of the first things I heard was the way everyone worked together recently to get the library open on time. And I understand you all participated in a home-rebuilding project to help a local family. That's the kind of dedication we need now. Let me run through the events quickly. One for each December weekend. Though the Chamber will mainly be responsible for the events in the first two."

Gemma shuffled the papers in front of her. "Week one will be the Dover Glory Lights kickoff, a special lighting ceremony to start the season. Instead of each store doing their own lights, there will be an overall plan for the downtown. All the lights will be hung on the buildings, over the streets around the square, and the decorations for the courthouse park will be set up. On Friday night, vendors will offer food and drink and at one point, all the lights downtown will go dark. Then we'll throw the switch and turn on all the decorations at once. It will be breathtaking. People will come from miles to see the large light display."

A woman on the aisle nodded. "That's true. We drive

all the way to Natchitoches, Louisiana, every year to see those lights along the Cane River."

"Exactly! And the second weekend in December will be our open-house weekend to showcase our businesses with our decorated windows. I'd like you each to be thinking of a way to create a Christmas window display that will evoke the spirit of the season and your company. There will be a contest for the top five windows. Visitors can vote here in town or online. Davis Blaylock at the *Dover Dispatch* is offering two months' free advertising for the winners."

A voice from the back called out, "I could sure use that."

Gemma spent the next forty-five minutes answering questions and assuring people that her weekend events could be accomplished with cooperation, minimum of cost and plenty of professional help. As she concluded the meeting she sensed excitement in the air. A swell of joy filled her throat. The owners were in agreement that pumping up the holiday events was vital to recuperating some of the sales lost when the Southways plant closed down last year and tossed over a hundred people out of work.

Several owners stopped by to express their delight in the events and pledge their support. Now it was up to her to make the necessary arrangements and coordinate all the bits and pieces.

"What happened to the Christmas parade?"

Gemma started at the sound of the deep voice. Linc's voice. It was hard to ignore once you'd heard it. Rich and smooth, it flowed along her nerves like warm honey. She looked into his blue eyes and suddenly found it difficult to swallow. "What are you doing here?"

"I've been in the back, listening to your pitch."

His intense navy blue eyes zeroed in on her, making her forget his question. "The parade?"

"It's a tradition. Has been since I was a kid. We all looked forward to it each year. There's going to be a lot of kids disappointed if it's canceled."

Linc's tone suggested that she should reinstate it at once. But she knew what he didn't. "I doubt that. According to the reports I have the parade has shrunk in size over the last five years, and attendance has fallen to a trickle." She tapped an app on her cell and swiped to the right page. "Last year there were only three floats, a fire truck and the Santa float. One police officer was assigned for crowd control and the parade lasted barely fifteen minutes." She smiled up at Linc. "Is that the tradition you're referring to?" A muscle in Linc's jaw flexed.

"I know you're new here and you're not familiar with our Christmas traditions. But we cherish our celebrations. We like the way it's been done in the past. It works for us."

She raised her chin and planted a hand on her hip. "Actually, it doesn't work. Business has fallen sharply over the past three years. When Southways closed it got worse. The Chamber has hired me to turn things around by making Christmas in Dover more appealing to people who will spend money in the stores and restaurants."

Linc crossed his arms and looked down his nose. "Surely you can come up with a compromise that will preserve our traditions and still attract tourists."

"Like a parade?"

"Yes. My mother was in charge of that for years and everyone loved it."

"Are you aware that there are six holiday parades around the area? Several in Jackson and the suburbs that are much larger and draw the bulk of the crowds. You have to give people more reason to come to Dover than just a puny parade."

"What if we don't want more people in Dover?"

"You're a businessman—is that what you really want?"

"What I want is to keep our cherished traditions intact."

"Traditions are habits with no meaning. Most people don't even know why or how they got started."

"You're wrong. They are important rituals that remind us of our past, of our roots and our history."

Gemma crossed her arms over her chest. "Really? Then, why does the courthouse put up a red star on the dome every year?" She almost laughed at the stunned look on Linc's face. He clearly had no answer for her. "It was donated to the city in 1972 to honor longtime mayor Louis Carswell. Is that part of the history you cherish?"

She scooped up her satchel and headed for the door, eager to make her escape while Linc was still stunned. He quickly caught up with her.

"You're deliberately twisting things."

She stopped and faced him. "No. I'm pointing out the flaw in your reasoning. Tradition is useless sentiment. Comfort food for the brain. I'm here to create events that will bring joy and happiness to people, to let them have fun and experience Christmas to the fullest."

"Are you talking about the commercial Christmas or the real one?

"Both."

"Not possible."

"Of course it is. If your heart is in the right place. Good night, Linc."

Gemma walked to her car with a smile on her face. She was actually coming to enjoy these little skirmishes with Linc. It might be fun toppling some of that arrogance.

What he didn't realize was that every time he challenged her it only made her more determined to make the Dover Christmas celebrations the biggest and flashiest she possibly could.

Take that, Mr. Linc.

Chapter Four

Saturday morning was chilly and overcast with a brisk breeze that demanded a warm jacket and a scarf to protect against the cold. Gemma hardly noticed. Her attention was focused on the happy boy on the field. Never had she felt so proud and so grateful. Watching Evan play flag football had lightened her mood and confirmed her decision to take the Chamber job. He was having the time of his life. He'd taken the field hesitantly at first, but quickly found his footing and had played the game with enthusiasm. It had helped that his new school friend and neighbor, Cody, was on the team.

And she had Linc to thank. She watched as he paced up and down the sidelines cheering on the boys, calling out directions and letting loose with a whoop and a fist in the air when they scored. He'd surprised her. She'd expected him to be demanding and harsh if the boys failed to perform well. When he strolled past her this time, he smiled and gestured toward the field.

"Evan is a natural. Was his dad an athlete?"

Gemma's good mood plummeted the way it always did when the subject of Evan's father came up. She stared straight ahead, focusing on the red number two on her son's back. "I have no idea." She sensed his surprise, but after a moment he moved on down the sideline calling out to one of the boys.

The game ended in a tie, but none of the players seemed to care. Evan raced toward her with a huge smile on his face, revealing his crooked teeth. There were braces in his future. But she'd do anything, spend any amount to make sure he had a happy life.

Linc dismissed the boys from a short postgame meeting, and Gemma opened her arms for a hug as soon as Evan ran back toward her. "You were great, honey. Did you have fun?"

"It was awesome. I can't wait for next week."

Linc joined them, ruffling Evan's hair. "Good job, buddy. You're a real asset to the team." He looked at her and smiled. "You ready to head to the storage area?"

They had ridden to the game with Linc this morning so he could show her the way. The fields were tucked away on the edge of Dover in what used to be a cotton field. She would have had trouble finding it alone. He also offered to drive her to the storage facility after the game.

"Yes. I just need to check with the Fenellis. They invited Evan to go with them to get pizza."

As soon as she climbed into Linc's truck she regretted agreeing to this arrangement. Evan had been with them this morning, and he and Coach, as Evan now called him, had discussed game strategy. Being alone with the man had her nerves firing and her palms sweaty—and had her questioning her lack of foresight. She stole a glance at her companion. No nerves there. He looked as cool as a cucumber, with his wrist resting on the steering wheel, eased back in the driver's seat and head cocked to one side as if he didn't have a worry in the world.

She suspected he did have things he was concerned

about. It wasn't hard to see that he grieved his father deeply. And her assistant, Leatha, had mentioned that with his brother Gil out of town, the entire company rested on Linc's shoulders. It was one of the largest electrical contracting firms in the area, with jobs stretching from Lake Charles, Louisiana, to Orange Beach, Alabama. She knew firsthand the stress of running a company, but Fine Day Events hadn't been nearly as large as Montgomery Electrical.

"So where is this storage facility located?"

"Across town. It used to be a drugstore before the owners sold it to the city. It got too hard to keep track of all the stuff needed for the events. Things kept getting lost, so Mom decided it would be easier to keep everything in one place."

"How long has your mom been doing the holiday events?"

"As long as I can remember. She used to help with all the fund-raisers, but that was before she opened up her real estate office."

He slowed and pulled into the lot of an old single-story building. He stopped near the door, jumped out and came around to her side before she could grasp the handle. Francie had obviously taught her son good manners. Unfortunately, personality wasn't something a parent could control. She slid out of the high truck, grateful for the narrow running board to help her down.

Linc opened the lock and stepped inside, switching on the overhead lights.

Gemma stared at the mess. Items were piled and tossed everywhere as if blindly thrown inside without regard to placement. "Oh, my."

Linc set his hands on his hips. "Looks as if we've

stepped into a scavenger hunt. Which way do you want to start?"

"I don't know. I have no idea what I'm looking for."

"Then, follow me. We'll start at the back and work our way forward."

Linc led the way, picking his steps through the narrow path on the floor. Gemma spotted the Christmas items first. "Linc, over there. Isn't that a red star?"

"Good eye." He shoved aside a large counter that resembled a lemonade stand with a sign above it reading Sidewalk Sale—Chamber Information. He lifted the six-foot-wide metal decoration and gave it a once-over. "I never realized how worn it was. It always looks shiny on the courthouse dome."

She sighed. If all the Christmas decorations were in the same poor shape, she'd spend a lot of time and money making them presentable.

Once the Christmas items were located she made a quick inventory. It looked as if a sizable part of her budget would go to buying lights and new decorations.

"Linc! Are you in here?"

"In the back."

Gemma glanced up as Tori made her way toward them, the frown on her face revealing her displeasure. "I saw your truck outside. Oh, hello, Gemma. What are y'all doing in here?"

"Looking for the Christmas decorations."

"I doubt if you'll find anything back here." Tori brushed dust off her jeans. "Mom was complaining last year that most of the stuff was falling apart and the city wouldn't cough up money for new ones."

Gemma stared at the odd assortment of rusty metal forms in the shape of trees and a set of faded and cracked oversize tree ornaments that she guessed were set on the courthouse lawn.

"I was hoping to find something that could be hung over the streets." She demonstrated with her hands. "You know—those drapes of lights that are hung overhead?"

Tori smiled and started rummaging through the junk. "I remember there used to be some with wreaths in the middle. It was really pretty, but I don't think Mom used them last year. Here's one." She pulled it up. "Ugh. It's a mess."

"I remember these." Linc set it out in the open space holding it upright with one hand while Gemma took a closer look.

It was a darling design. Exactly what she'd been looking for. But it needed a complete reworking. "How many are there?"

Linc and Tori did a quick count. "Looks like sixteen."

"Four for each street bordering the square. If we can repurpose these it would save a lot of money that could be spent on more lights for the storefronts." Gemma looked at Linc. "Do you know anyone who could fix these up and attach new lights?"

"I do." Tori smiled and nodded, sending her chin-length dark hair swaying. "Brother Seth. This is right up his alley. You should talk to him. I mean, we *do* own an electrical company. And I'll bet he'd do it for free, don't you think so, Linc?"

"Yeah. I guess. What are you doing here, exactly?"

"Oh. I need a ride to the airport Sunday afternoon. Mom said she'd be home this evening. I need to leave around five on Sunday."

Linc set the form aside, the scowl on his face deepening. "You need to stay here. Especially if Mom's coming home."

Tori mirrored the icy glare of her bother. Apparently it was a family trait. Gemma braced herself for the shouting match, a tightness forming in her chest. No matter how often her parents had fought and yelled, she'd never got used to it.

"Mom knows I'm going and she doesn't have a problem with it, so why do you?"

"Mom's not thinking clearly right now. Which means we all need to be here for her, not leaving her alone to deal with her grief."

"You don't get it. I doubt you ever will. Maybe if you'd ever been in love you'd understand."

"Tori, I could order you to stay."

"Are you serious? I'm twenty-six years old." She looked at Gemma. "It was nice seeing you again. Good luck with the events. I know they'll be great."

Linc stared after his sister a long while before shaking his head and looking at Gemma. "She's making a mistake. She's not thinking clearly."

"She seemed rational enough to me."

"So you're on her side?"

"I'm a stranger. I don't have a side, but yes, I understand what she's saying."

"Am I the only one who sees the need to band together now? To support Mom and help her get through Dad's passing. Family meant everything to him. Family *is* everything."

Gemma pressed her lips together. Maybe in his world. "Family is an accident of birth. We're handed a set parents and we have no say in the matter. Then we're expected to like it. Sometimes the only way to survive is to get out from under your family."

She dared a glance at Linc and, as she'd expected, the look of shock on his face said it all. Now he would start asking questions. Ones she wasn't about to answer. "I think I've seen all I need to here. We'd better go. I want to be home when the Fenellis bring Evan back." She moved quickly to the door and pushed it open, sucking in several deep breaths as she climbed into Linc's truck.

She'd been prepared for a shouting match to erupt between him and his sister, but they'd merely expressed differing opinions. Thankfully, because she'd had enough screaming and shouting to last her two lifetimes.

Linc slid into the driver's seat, handing her the key to the storage building. "Don't come over here alone. Bring someone with you."

It wasn't exactly an order, more of a stern warning, but Gemma bristled anyway. "You really like being in control of things. That's why you're so upset about my Christmas events isn't it? Because you have no say in anything I do."

He frowned. "No. That's not it at all. I just don't agree with your ideas."

Gemma smiled inwardly. She'd poked a hole in his "I know best" attitude and he didn't like it. She glanced at him. His formerly relaxed posture had become rigid and his irritation was evident in the way he rubbed his thumb against his forefinger as he clutched the steering wheel.

Her conscience reared its head. She shouldn't be so hard on him. Losing his father had been a shock, the most devastating loss of control a person could experience. "I'm glad you brought me here."

He looked over at her and nodded. "No problem."

Something in his tone triggered a realization. "You promised your mother you'd come with me, didn't you?"

He stopped the truck and looked at her in surprise. "How did you know?"

She stifled a grin and gave him a superior look. "I'm a mom. We know everything."

The scowl on Linc's face brought his dark brows together. She waited for him to respond, but he only huffed out a breath and drove out of the parking lot. He might be a big macho man on the outside, but inside he wasn't much different from Evan.

The realization pleased her a great deal.

The Montgomery dining room table held enough food to feed far more than the six people seated around the table Sunday afternoon. His mom had arrived home last night, and had spent the morning preparing all the family favorites. She'd ordered Linc to invite their new tenants to dinner. Gemma had been reluctant, but he'd finally convinced her that his mother would be very disappointed if she refused. But for some reason, she sat stiff and tense on the other side of Evan, who was equally braced as if waiting for something to happen. Linc passed the mashed potatoes to the boy, holding the heavy dish while he scooped out a helping then offering the dish to his mother.

Tori leaned forward and smiled at Gemma. "Have you told Seth about those old wreaths you found in storage?"

Gemma shook her head. "No, I haven't had a chance."

"Are you talking about the ones that used to hang over the street?" Francie passed the rolls to her daughter. "They're in terrible shape. That's why I haven't used them."

"What wreaths?" Seth glanced between the two women. Tori made a quick explanation.

"I'll bring them back to the shop and see what I can do. Should be fun. I'm looking forward to seeing more lights and decorations around town for the holidays."

Linc stabbed his roast to keep from expressing a contrary opinion. Apparently he was the only one in town who wanted things to stay the same. No one understood. The familiar events were comforting; the simplicity of the Dover celebrations kept the real meaning of Christmas in people's minds.

Gemma smiled at Seth. "Great, but you know we don't have much time."

Seth nodded. "I'll get right on it. As soon as I have them at the shop we'll get our heads together and see what we can do. What do you have in mind?"

Linc listened with growing irritation as Seth and Gemma bandied ideas back and forth across the table. His younger brother was a likable guy. Maybe too likable. He'd never been jealous of him, but suddenly he didn't like the idea of Gemma and Seth getting their heads together.

Seth suddenly pushed back from the table. "I hate to run, but I have to meet with a home owner this afternoon. She's not happy about where we put her breaker box." He winked and moved to kiss his mom goodbye.

"Aren't you staying for dessert?"

"I'll come back later. Save me a piece." He waved goodbye and hurried off.

Linc was about to ask about his mother's trip when he heard Evan inhale sharply. Milk from his overturned glass was soaking his mom's best tablecloth. Linc pushed back his chair. Evan winced and shrank away from him.

"I'm sorry. I'm sorry. I didn't mean to." Tears streamed down the boy's face.

Gemma pulled him close. "It's okay, sweetie. I'll clean it up."

Stunned, Linc exchanged a puzzled look with his mother. Why would a spilled glass of milk upset him so?

His mother reached out her hand to the boy and smiled. "Evan, come here, sweetheart." He glanced at her cautiously. "Come on. It's okay. I want to tell you a story."

Gemma nodded and released him. Slowly Evan went over to Francie's side. She wrapped her arms around his shoulders and hugged him close. "Don't you worry about that little spill. It's just milk. Do you see my boy over there?" Evan nodded, wiping his eyes as he looked at Linc. "Well, I know he looks big and strong now, but when he was your age, he spilled his milk every time he sat down at the table. No matter how hard he tried not to, it still happened. We tried moving his glass way back on the table. We tried using a big old mug instead of a glass. We even tried putting the glass on the sideboard, but he'd spill it carrying it to the table."

Evan almost smiled at that image. "Is that true, Coach?"

Linc wasn't about to tell the boy that his mother had seriously embellished the incident. "Pretty much. I was all elbows and extra fingers, it seemed."

Evan looked at Francie. "When did he stop?"

Tori chuckled. "He hasn't. He spilled his juice just this morning."

Linc smiled. Well, that was true enough.

"Linc, would you clean that up and bring this young man a fresh glass of milk? We're having chocolate cake for dessert. Do you like that?"

Gemma abruptly stood and hurried into the living room. Tori gestured for Linc to follow their guest while she cleaned up. He found Gemma standing near the fireplace, head bowed, arms wrapped around herself protectively. He couldn't be sure, but he suspected she was crying.

"Gemma, are you okay?"

She swiped at her eyes before facing him. "Yes. I just didn't expect… I mean, I wasn't prepared… Your mother was very kind and understanding."

He wasn't sure what she meant. "It was just a little spilled milk. The boy shouldn't be made to feel as if he'd done something wrong."

Her green eyes darkened. "You think I made him that way?"

"No, that's not what I said. He just seemed unusually upset over a minor thing."

"Minor? In my parents' home that would have been cause for punishment." She curled her fingers against her lower lip. "It's all my fault. I should have seen what was happening. I should never have gone back there."

"I don't understand."

Tori peeked in the room, interrupting their discussion. "Dessert is on the table."

Linc took Gemma's elbow and guided her back to the dining room. Evan was seated next to Francie munching down on a large piece of chocolate cake. He smiled up at them as they entered.

"Mom, I helped Miss Francie cut the cake and I carried all the plates to the table and didn't drop one."

Linc heard Gemma inhale sharply. "That's wonderful, Evan. I'm proud of you."

Settled beside Gemma at the table, Linc passed her a plate of cake, still trying to sort out Gemma's and Evan's odd behavior. She appeared calmer, but his curiosity was piqued. What kind of household had she grown up in? Twice now Gemma had made negative remarks about family. He'd grown up in a strong loving home. He knew not everyone was so blessed, that there were many dysfunctional families.

When the cake had been eaten, Gemma and Evan

quickly headed back to the cottage. He shut the door behind his departing guests, puzzling over their strange behavior. His mother's expression mirrored his thoughts.

"I wonder what that young woman has been through to make her so tense. Did she say anything to you?"

Linc shook his head. "Nothing that made sense. Something about how she should have seen what was happening."

Francie pursed her lips. "Something's not right there. I think the Lord has placed her here with us for a reason. We need to keep a close eye on them and see what we can do to help. I have a feeling they are both in serious need of love and attention."

Linc sensed the same thing, but he had no intention of acting upon them. Love and attention were his mother's area of expertise. Not his. And he had another, stronger feeling. That he'd be smart to steer clear of the lovely but confusing Gemma Butler.

Later that day, Gemma made her way out to the front porch and curled up in one of the wooden rockers. The best part of living in the cottage was the peace and solitude that surrounded the little house. And she craved both right now. The spilled milk incident at the mansion earlier still made her stomach quiver when she thought about it. Though it hadn't ended at all the way she'd expected.

Dining with the Montgomerys had made her tense and on edge. In her experience, family dinners usually ended in a verbal shouting match. So when Evan had knocked over his glass she'd been as stunned and frightened as her son. His heart-wrenching apology had twisted her stomach. She'd wanted to grab him and run back to the safety of their cottage. But Francie had responded with love and kindness. As she'd proceeded to tell Evan how Linc always spilled things as a child, Gemma had watched her son relax, leaning in against Francie as if drawing comfort from her grandmotherly hug. She'd even managed to restore Evan's confidence and good mood.

The love and understanding displayed before her had brought her to tears, and she'd taken refuge in another room. Though she still smarted from Linc's insinuation that she was the cause of her son's insecurity. She was beginning to see that his family was nothing like she'd experienced before. They met every situation with restraint and tolerance. There was no way they could understand her family's dysfunction.

Gemma glanced up as Francie came across the lawn in the fading light.

The woman smiled as she came up onto the porch. "Mind if I join you?"

"Please. I was just thinking about you. I never thanked you properly for what you did for Evan today."

"No need for that. The boy was upset over nothing. I've raised three boys, so I have a little more experience in dealing with them. Which is one of the reasons I'm here. Evan told me that you're picking him up from school each day, and then working from home."

"Yes. Why?"

"I know the job requires lots of face-to-face time with store owners and meetings with vendors. I have a suggestion. Evan and I hit it off. He's a sweet boy, and I have lots of time on my hands now. I'd be more than happy to watch Evan after school each day, for as long as needed."

"Oh, Miss Francie, that's really sweet of you, but that's too much to ask."

"Nonsense. It would fill my days. I'm used to having family around, but the children are grown and living their own lives. I'd hoped for grandchildren by now, but the only one I have was taken from us when she was a toddler. I'm praying that Gil will bring her back to us soon." Francie smiled and patted her arm. "You don't have to give me your answer now. But I'm sincere in this offer, and I think Evan and I can help each other."

The warmth behind the woman's offer tightened her throat. It was the perfect solution. "If you're sure it wouldn't be any trouble, then I'd like that. I'm sure Evan would, too."

"Wonderful." Francie stood, a big smile on her face. "Oh, and don't worry about ball practice. He can ride with Linc, and if he's working late I'll be happy to take him and watch the practice. I used to watch all the kids' games."

Gemma found herself envious of the loving mother Francie was. From what she'd seen, she'd raised fine upstanding children. Tori was friendly and feisty. Seth was kind and helpful. Gil was honorable—fighting for his child. She knew nothing of the sister in New York, but she was obviously pursuing her dream with her family's blessing. Linc—well, the jury was still out on Linc.

Chapter Five

Linc strode out of the office Tuesday morning and took the stairs down to the shop, heading toward the workroom in the back. Laughter floated on the air. A woman's laughter, and he thought he knew who it belonged to. But why was she here? He spotted Gemma and Seth huddled together in front of the workbench. Seth pointed to something on the surface and Gemma nodded enthusiastically. The rush of scalding heat sparking along his nerve endings caught him off guard.

"Hey, bro." Seth smiled and motioned him forward. "Come look at our project."

He moved closer, stopping beside Gemma and willing himself not to stare. She glowed with happiness. Her bright smile and sparkling eyes stole his breath. Her red-gold hair lay across her shoulder in one thick braid, contrasting with the blue sweater she wore over a denim skirt. Bright earrings bobbed against her neck as if mimicking her joy. His mouth went dry and he had to clear his throat to speak. "What project would that be?"

"The Christmas wreaths for the street drapes we found in the storage building?"

"Oh, right." He'd forgotten about those. He stole another quick glance at Gemma, then looked down at the table. The metal wreath looked nothing like the way it had before. The heavy-gauge metal frame had been covered with lights and some kind of green plastic that looked like a dismantled cheerleading pom-pom.

Seth nodded, a big smile on his face. "Watch this." He inserted the plug into the outlet, illuminating the decoration. "How's that? Pretty awesome, huh?"

Linc had to admit it looked better lit, but it still resembled something a third grader made from a coat hanger and tissue paper. He doubted expressing his honest opinion would contribute much at the moment. He searched for something noncommittal to say. "Looks good."

Gemma grinned. "Better than good. He transformed it. I'm thrilled."

Linc fought to ignore the way Gemma's delight washed through his senses, and eyed the strange-looking wreath. He couldn't imagine people flocking to Dover to see something so tacky hanging overhead. "So are they all going to look like this?"

"Oh, no." Gemma's smile widened. "Seth just put this together with things he had lying around. I'll order special green and red wrap to cover the frame. But the best part is it's not going to be very expensive to do all sixteen wreaths."

Linc couldn't take his eyes off her. She sparkled with enthusiasm. Was that all it took—an old restored wreath—to put this kind of joy in her heart? And she had his brother to thank. Not him. Why did that bother him? "So your budget won't take a hit, then?"

"Nope."

Seth unplugged the lights. "So what do you need, big brother?"

Linc had forgotten why he'd come downstairs. He'd

needed to vent. But not with Gemma here. "I was just getting out of the office."

Seth chuckled and nodded. "I hear you. I don't know how Dad could spend all day in that little box. I'd go crazy."

The mention of their father instantly dropped a heavy silence over the conversation. Gemma reached for her purse. "Well, thanks, Seth, for doing this. Any idea how long it'll take to complete the rest?"

"Couple days."

"Great. I meet with the business owners tomorrow. It'll help that I can report we've already started on the decorations. Thanks again. I really appreciate it."

"Any time."

Gemma faced Linc, slipping her bag over her shoulder. "Evan is looking forward to ball practice tonight."

"He's a good kid."

"I think so."

Linc watched Gemma walk out of the workroom, unable to wrest his attention from the soft swish of her braid across her shoulders as she moved. When she finally disappeared from sight, he released a quick breath. Every time he was near her she left some new indelible image in his mind. This time it was her radiant expression.

"Earth to Linc."

He jerked around to find his brother with a knowing grin on his face.

"She's a pretty lady, don't you think?"

No way was Linc going to go there with his little brother. But it did raise a question. Did Gemma find Seth attractive? They were about the same age, he guessed. His little brother was a charming guy. Linc could understand if Gemma was drawn to him. Not that it mattered to him. He gestured to the wreath frame. "This isn't going to take away from any of your jobs, is it?"

Seth's smile faded. "No. I get the feeling you aren't too happy with the changes Gemma plans to make."

"I think it's a waste of time and money, and I doubt it'll make any difference in the long run."

"Really?" Seth crossed his arms over his chest. "I think you're wrong, but I guess time will tell. So what's up with you? Something on your mind?"

Linc set his hands on his hips. "The Coleman bid. I have a bad feeling about it. I wish Gil could have worked up the calculations."

Seth patted his arm. "No worries. Montgomery Electric rarely loses those big bids. Everyone knows we're the best in the business."

"I hope you're right."

Seth set the wreath aside. "Have you talked to him about it? You did send him the final figures before you submitted the bid, right?"

Linc leaned a hip against the counter. "Yeah, but he was distracted. I don't think he looked very closely."

"He's got a lot on his mind."

"I know. But so do I." None of his family understood the tremendous burden he'd assumed at the company. The only one who would understand was gone.

Linc made his way back to the office, thoughts of Gemma pushing into his mind again. He wondered if she'd come with Evan to the ball field to watch practice. He hoped so. Though having her on the sidelines might not be a good idea. Whenever Gemma was around he was easily distracted by her animated presence.

Hoping to block thoughts of his lovely tenant, Linc placed a call to his brother Gil, looking for a little reassurance that the bid he'd submitted was on target. "You sure those figures were in line with the work they want done?"

"Don't worry. It's okay. I'm sorry I couldn't be there to look at it more closely, but I just can't leave Mobile right now. Every time I turn around there's a new legal hoop to jump through."

Linc's former sister-in-law had put his brother through emotional torture after their divorce, finding countless ways to keep him from their adopted daughter. "But you'll get Abby back, won't you?"

"Yeah, but there's a lot to untangle first, and the court system here moves like a slug."

"You can fill us in at Thanksgiving." His brother's lack of response made him uneasy.

"I don't think so. Leaving town might mess things up. Abby's been through a lot and I need to be here with her. You understand, don't you?"

"Yeah. Sure. You do what you have to do. We'll be praying for you. But come home as soon as you can. Mom's aching to see Abby again."

"I know. I want her back home, too."

Linc ended the call, then rested his elbows on the desk, grasping the back of his neck with his hands. Never in his life had he felt so alone and abandoned. His dad and his brothers had been his anchor. But Dad was gone and Gil was stuck in Mobile. Linc had been looking forward to Thanksgiving with the family as a way to reconnect and gain strength and support from those he loved. But it might be a smaller gathering than usual this year.

Fighting off the swell of grief pressing against his ribs, he swiveled back to the computer and pulled up the next construction project. His best course of action now was to make sure Montgomery Electrical had plenty of jobs lined up for the future. He couldn't bring his father back, but he could ensure the legacy he'd cherished.

Gemma gathered her hair up on the top of her head and stared at the lighting fixture above her dining room table. She'd been on the job only ten days and she was already facing a major glitch. And for once she wasn't sure how to proceed. It was at times like this that she missed Darren. Before his betrayal they'd been a great brainstorming team. It was one of the things that had made Fine Day Events a success. Lowering her arms, she propped her elbows on the table. She needed advice.

Time to get another point of view, and who better to ask than the woman who'd directed Christmas in Dover for over a decade? Scooping up her cell, she dialed the main house and was relieved when the older woman answered.

"Gemma, dear. How are you? Is everything all right?"

"Yes, but I do have a problem I'd like to discuss with you if you have some time."

"Has Linc been giving you trouble?"

Why in the world would she even ask that? "No. It's about the Christmas decorations for the square."

"Oh. Fine. Are you at the office or at home today?"

"I'm here at the cottage."

"I'll be there in about six minutes. I'm waiting to take the last batch of cookies from the oven."

Gemma smiled as she placed her cell back on the table. Since Francie had been watching Evan there had been an increase in the amount of homemade cookies and cupcakes coming from the Montgomery kitchen. Francie said it soothed her and made her feel grounded to provide warm treats for Evan, and it reminded her of when her own kids were all home.

She tried to imagine Linc as a small boy, but it was hopeless. No way could she see the strong, masculine eldest son as anything other than full grown. Maybe she'd ask Francie to show her a picture sometime.

Within minutes Francie was tapping on the front door. She stepped inside with a smile and a warm plate of cookies. "I always discuss better with fresh cookies, don't you?"

"Ooh, they smell wonderful."

"Old-fashioned oatmeal. Linc's favorite. I put raisins in them once and he pitched a fit." She chuckled. "I never did it again. Unless I was making a batch for Bethany. She always wanted nuts and raisins in hers."

"Did you make a special batch for each child?"

"Sometimes." She nodded. "It's what moms do."

Gemma took a warm cookie from the plate, marveling at the scope of her friend's love. Her mother had never baked a cookie in her life. What would it be like to have someone make your favorite cookies especially for you? The soft cookie melted in her mouth. "Francie, these are scrumptious!"

"Thanks." She glanced down at the sketches and papers spread out on the table. "So what do you need to talk about?"

Gemma pointed to the two calendars in the center. November and December. "We have a problem and I'm not sure how to handle it." She pointed to the Thursday with the star in the corner. Thanksgiving. "Notice anything odd about November?"

Francie looked at the date, slowly shaking her head. "Oh! Thanksgiving is early this year. We have a week before the start of December."

Gemma tugged her hair behind her ears. "This can either be a good thing or a bad thing. I'm not sure which."

"How so?"

"I've started ordering decorations for the courthouse park and scheduling people to hang the street drapes and the lights on the storefronts, but they can't guarantee them before Thanksgiving because of short notice. Plus, most of what I need can't be delivered until after the holiday. Traditionally, the day after Thanksgiving is the kickoff for Christmas events, but I'm going to need that week to decorate. There's simply not enough time to get things ready before then. I'm not sure what to do. The day after Thanksgiving is Black Friday, one of the busiest days in retail. Won't people be expecting everything to be set up by then?"

Francie stared at the calendar. "Normally, yes. But this year is different. The Chamber knew it was giving you a narrow timeframe. And truthfully, Black Friday isn't that big a deal in Dover. The majority of folks go up to the malls in Jackson or the big-box stores in Sawyer's Bend."

Gemma sank into the chair. "I thought that might be the case. I was looking at sales figures from last year and there's not much of a jump on Black Friday. So I was thinking, what if we took that lame-duck week and used it as our decorating time? I can schedule everything for the first of the week. We can get the lights hung, the park decorated, the trees set up, and we'll be ready to kick off the first weekend in December as planned."

"I think that's a perfect solution."

"That's a relief. I just needed to make sure I was thinking it through logically. You don't think the merchants will object?"

"Not at all. They all want the same thing. We need to put Dover on the map, bring in new business and new interest. You do what you think best. That's why I recommended you."

"Thanks, Francie. I really appreciate your help."

The older woman patted her arm. "That's what I'm here for."

A knock on the front door brought Gemma to her feet. Linc stood on her porch, hands on hips, eyes narrowed in concern. "Is my mom here?"

Gemma motioned him in.

"Linc? What's wrong?" Francie looked over her shoulder at her son.

"I came home and didn't know where you were. I smelled cookies, but you weren't in the house."

"I brought Gemma some cookies. We had things to discuss about the Christmas events."

Linc looked between them. "Yeah, well, you left the oven on, Mom."

"Oh, dear." She lifted her shoulders in chagrin, and chuckled. "That's a bad habit of mine. I love to bake, but I get distracted, then I end up with burned cookies instead of chewy ones. Dale used to get so frustrated with me…" She stopped abruptly, her hand coming to rest in the center of her chest. Her eyes grew moist. "I'd better go see to that stove."

"I already did, Mom."

"Good. Thank you, dear. Gemma, we'll talk later." She hurried out the door.

She closed the door watching through the glass pane in the center as the older woman made her way slowly across the lawn. Her earlier energy was gone, bringing an ache to Gemma's heart. "Will she be all right?"

Linc spoke from behind. "I hope so. I only wish I knew what to do for her."

Gemma pivoted to face him, coming up short when she realized how close he stood. She eased back a step and looked up into his concerned expression. He loved his mother deeply. "I'm not sure there's anything you can do. Just be there and love her." A flash of sadness darted through his eyes. She tore her gaze from his and stepped around him. "Would you like a cookie? Francie said they're your favorite."

Linc took a couple from the pile in his hand, one corner of his mouth lifting. "She hasn't made these in a long time. She's started baking again since she's been watching Evan."

"Evan looks forward to spending time with her. I think they are good for each other."

"I suppose so. So what's going on with the Christmas events? Mom giving you advice on how to do things?"

She ignored his challenging tone. "There's an extra week between Thanksgiving and the first of December. We decided to use that to decorate the downtown."

"But Christmas always starts the day after Thanksgiving. Everyone knows that. It's—"

Gemma raised her hand as she sat back down at the table. "Tradition. I know. But not this year. There's not enough time to get everything in place. We'll need that entire week to prepare for the Dover Glory Lights event."

Linc placed his fisted knuckles on the tabletop and stared down at her. "That's a big mistake. No one is going to be happy about pushing Christmas kickoff back a week."

Gemma smiled up at him, inwardly bracing against the waves of emotion emanating from Linc. He may appear cool on the outside, but inside he felt things fiercely. "It can't be helped. A little speed bump, nothing more. Besides, your mother thinks it won't be an issue, and she should know."

He straightened, shaking his head slightly. "Why are

you so determined to change everything? Our Christmas has been just fine for a long time."

She ignored the way he loomed over her and focused on her job. "Just fine until Southways closed. You might not have noticed a drop in business since then, but the merchants on the square have. They need to revitalize the downtown, draw more customers."

"By turning our simple Christmas into a spectacle? Hasn't the holiday been hijacked enough with people ignoring the real reason for Christmas, calling it a holiday, turning it into a greedfest? I want better for my hometown." Linc gestured to the papers on the table. "I don't suppose this speed bump means you'll have to scale back on your Rockefeller-style extravaganza?"

If she wasn't so irritated she would have laughed out loud. He was behaving like a little boy who didn't get to hang the star on the treetop. "Not at all. In fact, I should have the time now to add those extra touches I've been thinking about. And by the way, the whole world flocks to Rockefeller Center to enjoy the lights."

Linc leaned down and looked into her eyes. "And by the way, this isn't New York."

His smile was mocking, and his eyes were filled with a challenging glint. His nearness sent her nerve endings dancing. Gemma swallowed her discomfort. "That's a good thing, because I don't have the budget for that many lights." She held her ground, wondering what he would do next. She expected him to storm out. Instead, he shoved his hands in his back pockets and shook his head.

"Don't you have any traditions that you cherish, or are you a female Scrooge who hates Christmas?"

Gemma looked away. There'd never been consistent traditions in her family, unless you counted the lack of tradition as one. She stood and faced him, arms crossed over her chest. "I love Christmas. I love the reason we celebrate, I love the music, the decorations and the gifts. I love the nativity scenes and the trees, but mostly I love the lights. I want lights from every rooftop, every tree and shrub and building and walkway. I want to make downtown Dover as beautiful and glorious as possible. Yes, the lights will draw in visitors, the more the better. But I don't think of them as glamorizing the holiday, but a way to draw them to Christ. If we wanted to show people the real meaning of Christmas, how the light of His life changed the world, then we couldn't put up enough lights on the planet." She took a deep breath, brushing her hair behind her shoulder. She'd gotten carried away. She dared a look at Linc, prepared for whatever rebuttal he was going to toss her way. Instead, she found a puzzled frown on his face and an odd light in his blue eyes that only added to her unease.

The air between them vibrated the way it always did when he was near, but this was different, softer. As if he was seeing her in a different way. She held her breath. When he remained silent she plunged ahead.

"And as for Santa, he's the symbol of giving. God gave us Himself and taught us how to give to others. Each time we give a gift we're honoring Him. I want people to come to Dover and rejoice. Maybe some of them will go home and want to learn about Jesus."

The scowl on Linc's face eased into a small smile. Her heart rate quickened and a surge of anxiety chilled her veins. She didn't know what she'd said that had caused the shift in attitude, but the warmth in his eyes had warmed her blood several degrees.

Linc's shoulders relaxed. "Well, when you put it like that…"

She thought he would say more, but he picked up another cookie from the plate and nodded. "I'd better check on Mom."

Gemma breathed a sigh of relief when he shut the door behind him. Unfortunately, he'd left plenty of his vibrant energy behind. They were on opposite sides of the holiday issue, but she found herself enjoying the sparring between them. She always felt alive and strong. Not that she'd bested him, but that she'd held her own. It was nice to know her old determination was coming back. And that was all it was. It certainly had nothing to do with the strong-jawed, blue-eyed, all-male eldest son. Not at all.

She was not attracted to him. She was not.

Gemma sorted through her papers and notes Thursday evening as she waited for the town square business owners to arrive. This was their second meeting and the most important. She would lay out detailed plans for the various activities. She'd taken photos of the refreshed wreaths Seth was working on, which she posted on a corkboard behind her. She hoped the quick progress would inspire the owners and nudge those who might be on the fence to get on board.

She'd accomplished a lot in the past two weeks. She'd upgraded the Dover website, solicited food vendors for the weekends and started contacting local media about the upcoming events. Her only concern was how the owners would feel about that lame-duck week when they'd have to decorate. Mayor Bill Ogden was on board so she didn't think it would be a problem, but as Linc had pointed out, she was tampering with tradition and that could spell problems.

The conference room door creaked and her spirits dipped when she saw Linc walk in. "What are you doing here?"

"I'm a business owner."

"True, but you don't own a business on the square."

"No, but Mom made me promise to help you out. So here I am."

"She did not."

A sly smile moved his lips. "She did. You can ask her."

"Well, you can tell Francie I appreciate her concern, but I don't need your help."

Linc set his hands on his hips and shrugged. "Doubt if that'll work, but you're welcome to talk to her when you see her."

Gemma busied herself with her handouts, sorting them in piles and laying them crisscrossed, and trying to ignore Linc. He was probably right. Francie would be offended if she refused her son's help. She no doubt saw it as a kind gesture. Gemma saw it as an obstacle she didn't need.

"Fine. Then, take a seat and don't interrupt. I have a lot to cover and I don't need any negativity from you."

"No problem. There'll be plenty of negativity once everyone gets here."

Gemma sent a scowl in his direction, which only made him smile. He took a seat on the end of the first row, right in her line of sight. If he thought he was going to intimidate her, he had a surprise coming. Once she was focused on her task, nothing could pull her out of the zone.

Linc sat, spread his arms out along the back of the chairs, rested one ankle on his knee and grinned. Gemma's pulse quickened and a warm flush filled her cheeks. She pulled her gaze away, allowing her hair to fall forward and hopefully hide her reaction. Okay, so she could focus when it was anyone but him. The dark jeans and cream-colored Henley that he wore did little to hide the sculpted chest and muscled arms. The sleeves were shoved up, revealing corded forearms and a black watch strapped across his wrist. He looked relaxed, confident and defiant. He was taunting her, biding his time until the other owners arrived and started poking holes in her plans.

No way. She would not let him influence the others who were starting to arrive. Quickly she went to greet them and introduce herself to the ones who'd missed the previous meeting. When she returned to the front of the room, she was able to ignore Linc and focus on the job at hand. Well, almost.

"Good evening. I'm so glad to see so many of you here. We have a lot to go over and I know you'll have questions." She explained about the extra week and her plans for decorating. When no one expressed any concerns she moved forward.

Gemma briefly went over the plans for the grand lighting the first weekend and explained about the lamppost-decorating contest, and the addition of carriage rides around the square.

"Oh, how romantic." A woman in the front row smiled up at her.

Gemma smiled in agreement, her confidence lifting a notch. "Week three will be the children's weekend. We will continue with your lovely tradition of having visitors donate toys, and I understand Peace Community Church will host that event. The annual community dinner will be held again, but that is organized by the city of Dover. Santa will be enthroned in the square park to visit with the children, and street vendors will be offering food and beverages. This will give visitors a chance to wander along the storefronts and cast their vote for the best windows." Gemma sent a smug smile in Linc's direction.

"Sounds like a lot of work to me." An older man in the third row stood. "I'm Denver Kolb. I can decorate the window, all right. My wife's good at that sort of thing, but how are we going to get folks to come down here? How are they going to hear about our newfangled celebrations?"

"I've already started on that. Thankfully, Dover already has a very appealing website. I've added a page for our Christmas events and will post pictures as we go along. I've also started to contact various media outlets—newspapers, television, radio—to let them know what we are doing. But the best marketing tool we have is you. Word of mouth will draw more people to Dover than any other thing. Talk it up to your friends, your relatives. Post it on your social media pages."

"I don't do any of that social stuff. Do you have anything I can give people?"

"I will have something, yes. I'm working on a small postcard-size handout and a large poster that you can place in various places. I should have all of this finalized in a day or so. I will keep in touch with you via email, or if that's not an option, Leatha will call you and leave messages."

"What about the last weekend? Will it still focus on the real meaning of Christmas?"

Gemma stole a quick glance at Linc and saw a faint smirk on his lips. She squared her shoulders and smiled out at the crowd. "Yes. Absolutely. The local choirs will still sing, and the churches on the square will be open for prayer or candlelight services. We'll keep the food vendors and hopefully the carriage rides, but that weekend will be devoted to honoring the season."

She swallowed around the tightness in her throat, waiting for the reactions to her plans. "I know this sounds like a lot of things to pull together, but most of it will fall on me. I've done this before, many times, and I've organized events that will deliver the greatest impact for the least amount of effort. Provided we all work together. I'm here to help you work through your concerns and tackle issues as they arise, but I don't think there will be any we can't handle together."

The owners stood and began chatting, many of them approaching her with questions and comments. To her relief, most were enthusiastic and excited about the events and no one expressed concern about that extra week.

Linc strolled up to the table where she'd laid her drawings. She squared her shoulders and smiled. "So. I guess you were disappointed."

He frowned. "'Bout what?"

"That the owners didn't rebel against my plans for the events or the lame-duck workweek. I thought they were very cooperative and even enthusiastic."

"We'll see." He inhaled a slow breath. "I know you believe in what you're doing. I get that, but I'm concerned about the long-term. Part of the charm here is the low-key way we do things. These events will change the focus. Instead of sitting back and enjoying the holiday, we'll be running around trying to top last year, and Christmas will be lost in trying to make things bigger and flashier."

The man was determined to keep Dover in the last century. "Well, it's fortunate that you're not the one in charge, then, isn't it?"

A woman approached and Gemma took the opportunity to turn away from Linc. "Can I help you?"

"I'm Shirley Roe from the Magnolia Diner. I couldn't make the first meeting, but I wanted to tell you how excited I am about expanding our holiday events. I know the increase in visitors will be a blessing for my business. Most of the people at Southways ate lunch at my place. I'm planning on doing a little sprucing up before the big lighting weekend. I want our visitors to see the real charm of my café and the down-home food we offer."

"That's wonderful. I'm going to do my best to make sure these weekends are as special as they can be."

Shirley extended her hand. "Thank you, Mrs. Butler, or do you prefer Ms.?"

Gemma grasped the woman's hand. "Gemma is fine."

Linc was still standing near the table, studying her with his intense blue eyes. She raised her chin. "Another satisfied customer."

"So which is it? Ms. or Mrs.?"

A twinge of anger tightened her throat. What did it matter? But maybe she could shut down his curiosity with the truth. "Miss. I've never been married." She saw the surprise register in his eyes and the sudden tightening of his jaw. In for a penny in for a pound. "And yes, Evan is my biological child. Any other questions?"

Linc had the grace to look embarrassed. "I didn't mean to pry."

"Yes, you did." Gathering up her papers, she slipped them into the satchel and headed for the door. Why did everyone think they had a right to ask personal questions? *Where's your husband? Are you widowed? Divorced?* Sometimes she wanted to silence them all with the truth, but that would only create more questions.

She could feel Linc's eyes on her back as she left the room. What was he thinking? No doubt his estimation of her had changed. It didn't matter. He was only the son of her landlord. He had no power over her at all.

Inside her car she buckled up and turned the ignition key. So why did she want him to have a good opinion of her? It made no sense. Though, he was a member of one of the most influential families in Dover. Having his support would be a blessing. But she had Francie behind her, which was more important. Linc was just an irritating gnat she'd have to deal with.

A gnat that refused to vacate her thoughts. He slipped in at the oddest moments. Her only hope was to stay so busy that she had no time to think of anything else. She had a lot to do if she was going to succeed.

Chapter Six

The stars were out and the temperatures dipping into the forties as Linc steered his truck toward the garage behind the main house. He'd been delayed by friends at the meeting who were all eager to express their delight over the new Christmas events. He'd tried to keep his personal opinions to himself, but it had been difficult. Gemma had made the whole upgrade of Christmas sound like a birthday party. He'd left feeling irritated and short-circuited as he always did when he was around her.

She stirred up unwelcome emotions and made observations that left him feeling exposed and vulnerable. Like when she'd called him on his need to be in control. It was true. With Dad gone, he felt he'd lost all control of his life. Gemma's tampering with Dover's Christmas celebrations was adding insult to injury.

However, her heartfelt explanation of the Christmas lights last night had moved him and forced him to look at the decorations from a new perspective. It had also cracked open a place in his heart he'd not visited for a long while. Since his last relationship had ended, he'd shut down all romantic feelings. Gemma was nudging them to life again. Even though he'd fought against it, he'd been attracted to her from the start. She wasn't like any woman he'd met before. Gemma was creative, impulsive, changed things on the fly. He couldn't pin her down.

But her comments about family, traditions, and now her statement about her marital situation made him wonder if they shared the same values.

In the garage, Linc pulled his Chevy truck to a stop beside his dad's battered Ford pickup. His heart twisted with a bittersweet memory. Dad was a Ford man to the core and had jokingly complained about having Linc's bow tie monster parked so close. Gil had threatened to buy a Dodge just to irk their dad even more. Now Linc looked at the silent vehicle and wondered what would happen to it. Mom had her own small car. She had no use for the old truck.

By the time Linc entered his kitchen a few moments later, his mood had soured further. Each day he awoke, he felt as if a large chunk of his heart had been ripped away. He'd moved back home to watch over his mother and he was glad he'd done so. Whether she realized it or not, she needed someone close by.

"How did the meeting go, sweetheart?"

His mother was seated at the breakfast table dressed in her bathrobe and slippers, a hot cup of tea and her e-reader in front of her. It was barely after nine in the evening. She never went to bed before eleven and never changed into her pajamas until she was ready to sleep. Maybe she was sick. The thought lanced through him like a knife. He couldn't survive losing another parent. "Mom, are you all right?"

"Of course. Why do you ask?"

Easing into a chair, he searched his mother's face for some clue as to what was bothering her. "You're in your robe and drinking hot tea."

She smiled as understanding dawned. "Oh. I see. There's nothing wrong. I'm just tired and I thought I'd turn in early. Evan and I played games most of the evening." She patted his hand. "So tell me about the meeting."

Linc chewed the inside of his mouth as he tried to organize his thoughts. "It went okay, I guess. Just not the way I expected."

"Oh?"

He leaned forward, resting his arms on the table. "Everyone is all fired up and I don't get it."

"You mean they didn't like Gemma's ideas?"

"No, they loved them. That's what I don't get. I figured everyone would see the damage these changes could do and refuse to go along with them."

"And they didn't?"

"No. They were all jumping for joy, like everything we've done in the past was meaningless." He stood and went to the refrigerator, pulled out the pitcher of sweet tea and poured a glass. "How many times have we talked about the overcommercialization of Christmas? The loss of the spiritual meaning. Now all of a sudden the town wants to dump our traditions for all the glitz."

"And this bothers you?"

"Of course. Traditions are important."

"What exactly is Gemma proposing?"

He shook his head; once his mom heard some of Gemma's weird ideas she'd be on his side. "First, she wants all the businesses around the square to decorate their windows as part of a contest she's promoting on the Dover website to draw in visitors to see the winners. She even got Davis to offer free advertising in the *Dispatch* for the winners."

"Interesting. Is that all?"

"No. There's a lamppost-decorating contest, too, that anyone can enter." Linc leaned back in his chair. "Screwy idea if you ask me."

"How did folks respond?"

He thought back to the moment when Gemma had finished her discussion and the owners had applauded. Loudly. They'd crowded around her afterward with questions and smiles "As if she'd just offered them each a free trip to Disney World."

Francie took a sip of her tea before answering. "I think her ideas are right on target."

"You can't be serious."

"She's doing what she was hired to do, and it sounds as if the owners are all eager to participate. I knew she would charm them. She's so full of enthusiasm, don't you think?"

Linc didn't want to discuss his reactions to Gemma. He still hadn't figured out why he became all edgy and irritable when she was around.

"I enjoy helping her out by watching Evan after school. It gives her more time to concentrate on her new job."

"Are you sure he's not too much for you? I mean, he's an energetic little kid."

"I look forward to having him here each day. You know how much I've longed for grandchildren, and I haven't had Abby around since she was small. Besides, he needs a grandma and I need a little childishness in my life. Will it bother you having Evan around the house?"

"No. He's a great kid. It's just…we're getting pretty tangled up with our tenants. I'm not sure that's such a good idea."

"We get tangled up in all of our friends. Or is there something different about Gemma and Evan? Like perhaps she's very attractive and very single?"

Linc held up a hand to ward off further conversation. "No. She is not my type. She's one of these women that want to do everything on their own. Job. Career. Even kids. They don't need the messy complications of falling in love, getting married and then starting a family. Just jump to the end."

"I don't understand."

"She told me tonight she has never been married."

"I see. And so you jumped to the conclusion that she's antimarriage and family?"

"That, and from some of the other things she's said about family and traditions." He carried his glass to the sink.

"Well, I'm sure there's some logical explanation. I know her fairly well and I can't see her being a die-hard feminist the way that one girlfriend of yours was." Her eyes narrowed. "Is that why you broke up with Kelsey last year? Was she too new-century for you?"

Linc set his jaw. "That was only part of it. We didn't want the same things. I wanted a family and she wanted her career."

"And how about Tina? What was wrong with her?"

He was in no mood to analyze his past relationships with his mother. Linc winked and kissed his mother on the cheek. "She wasn't you." He stopped at the kitchen door when she called his name.

"That's not the first time you've said that to me. Do you mean that? Are you looking for a woman like me?"

"Of course. You're beautiful, strong, smart and funny. The perfect combination."

"Linc. I'm flattered. But you shouldn't be looking for a clone of me." She stood and came to him. "You should be looking for the woman God has chosen for *your* life."

"You and Dad had the perfect marriage. That's what I want, and I'm not going to settle for anything less."

His mother touched his arm lightly. "Your father and I had a wonderful life together, but you're only seeing the last twenty years. You didn't see the years when we struggled, when he worked late and I never saw him, when we fought over money and how to discipline you kids. We worked at making our marriage strong. It didn't start out that way and it bothers me that you think so."

"I know marriage takes work. But I'm not settling for someone who isn't right." Linc saw sadness fill his mother's eyes. "I'm sorry if I upset you, Mom. I just want lasting love like you and Dad had. He was a lucky man to have someone like you who made him happy every day."

His mother's eyes clouded over and her shoulders sagged. "Did I make him happy every day?"

"Of course. You made each other happy." The sadness and doubt in his mother's eyes tugged at his heart.

"I hope so." She picked up her e-reader and clutched it to her chest. "I'm turning in. I'll see you in the morning."

Linc watched his mom walk away with a heavy heart. He wasn't sure what he'd said to disturb her, but since his father's death, she reacted oddly to many things. As deeply as he grieved, he couldn't begin to imagine the pain of losing a spouse of thirty-nine years.

He turned out the lights in the kitchen and made his way to his room. The silence in the house pressed in on him. Dad had been a night owl, staying up late to either work or watch *SportsCenter* and get caught up on his favorite teams. The lack of noise emphasized the giant hole inside him that his father had once filled.

Climbing into bed, he stared at the ceiling. He missed his dad's wise council now. His dad would know how to keep the family together and the company running. He'd probably have some sound advice on what to do about Gemma, too.

Pressure began to build deep in his gut, moving upward, pressing against his ribs with tremendous force. Covering his eyes with his forearm, Linc gave in to his grief.

Crisp Saturday-morning air blew strands of hair across Gemma's cheek. She ignored it. Fingers pressed against her mouth, she held her breath, her heart stilled as Evan cut sharply to the right, avoiding the grasping hands of another player, and charged toward the goal line, scoring a touchdown that won the game. Evan slammed the ball to the ground and jumped up and down, a huge smile on his face.

A shout of triumph from Linc distracted her. His usual scowl was gone, replaced with a heart-melting smile that softened his sharp features and raised his handsome quotient several notches. It increased her pulse rate, too. She watched as Linc jogged across the field, gathering his players like little chicks and handing out high fives and hugs. When he got to Evan, he scooped him up in a bear hug before setting him down and ruffling his hair.

Gemma didn't know which sight pleased her more: her son's happy smile or the pride reflected in Linc's deep blue eyes. Both were a sight to behold, and both were images she thought she'd never see. This was Evan's third ball game, and the second they'd won. Evan was consumed with playing flag football. Being part of the team had accomplished more than she'd ever dreamed.

Francie Montgomery came to her side. "What a great game. Evan is thoroughly enjoying himself."

Unable to speak around the lump in her throat, she nodded, fighting back tears. Who would have thought that Evan would blossom under someone like Linc? A man she thought she'd never want to know.

"And I think my boy is enjoying himself, too. It's good to see him having fun. Linc is far too serious. Your son is good for him."

Gemma glanced at her friend. It was odd to hear her speak of Linc as her boy. There was nothing boyish about him. But she supposed when Evan was full grown she'd still think of him as her boy, too, no matter how masculine he was. "He's very good with the kids. Very patient. I hadn't expected him to be." She clamped her mouth shut. Francie was such a good friend that she'd forgotten she was also Linc's mother.

Francie chuckled softly. "You expected him to be stern and disapproving?"

"I guess."

"Linc can be a hard man to get to know. He keeps his emotions buried deep. People often think he's cold and distant, but he's not really. He's always been reserved. Unfortunately, losing his dad has made him more withdrawn. Coaching this team has helped him ease up a bit."

"Evan adores him. You, too."

"Well, the feeling is mutual. You've raised a special boy. Not easy when you're a single parent."

"No. Sometimes I feel as if I've failed him completely." Logically she knew many single mothers raised fine, upstanding children all alone. But she wanted more for Evan. A traditional home with a traditional family. But she didn't believe it would ever happen.

Linc and the team of happy children spilled out over the edge of the field, meeting up with parents and receiving hugs and congratulations. Evan took the sports drink she offered him and downed half. His face was red from running, his cheeks streaked with dirt, but it was the happiest she'd seen him in nearly a year. She reached out and hugged him, only to have him pull away.

"Aw, Mom. I'm too big for that stuff."

Gemma didn't know whether to laugh or cry.

Francie shared a high five with Evan before he trotted off to talk to a friend. "Don't be too upset. He'll still let you hug him, just not in public. Don't tell anyone, but I still hug Linc each morning. He hates it, but he endures it."

Gemma glanced at Linc. She remembered the solid feel of those strong arms around her that day when she'd nearly tumbled off the porch. The warmth and security she'd experienced in his embrace. Linc suddenly turned and looked directly at her, a smile reflected in his eyes. Heat flushed into her neck. He raised his head and winked. Arrogant man. Gathering up Evan's belongings, she said goodbye to the parents she'd come to know, eager to get to the car and put distance between herself and the far too compelling coach.

She'd been so busy this week she hadn't seen Linc until he walked out on the field this morning. The sight of him had made her heart jump. The same way it had just now when he'd caught her staring. Embarrassed, she ducked her head, keeping her attention on Evan.

Settled in the car, Gemma wrinkled her nose. "Evan. You stink."

"Gee, thanks, Mom."

A rainstorm had passed through yesterday and the combination of muddy playing field and little-boy sweat permeated the car. She started to remind him to shower as soon as they got home, but then she looked at his still-shining eyes. "I'm so proud of you. That was amazing the way you dodged that other boy and scored."

"Mr. Linc and I worked on that play."

Linc. He was becoming more and more a part of their lives and that made her uncomfortable. Sooner or later they would leave the cottage and she'd take a job elsewhere. How would Evan deal with that?

"Mom. Can I give Miss Francie a birthday party?"

Gemma stole a quick glance at her son. "What brought this on?"

"She asked me when mine was and she said hers is on Wednesday. I want to give her a party to show her how much I like her."

"That's very sweet, Evan, but that's not much time to organize. Besides, she might have other plans."

"No. All her kids 'cept Mr. Linc and her other boy aren't home. She'll be really lonely. Please, Mom?"

An old memory burned in her chest, heating the blood in her veins. She'd had a similar idea when she was Evan's age. One that had ended in disaster and still pained her after all these years. "Who do you want to invite?"

"You and me. Coach and his brother, and Miss Caroline."

It was typical of her son to include people he cared about. Gemma considered his request. Why not? Only six people. She could make a cake, serve ice cream and coffee. Keep it simple. She loved to entertain but rarely had the chance. "I suppose we could check with her."

"No. It has to be a surprise. I have it all worked out, but I need help with the cake and stuff and you'll have to call everyone."

Gemma slowed to make the turn into the Montgomery drive. Francie had taken Evan to practices this past week since Gemma had been consumed with the myriad details in getting the events organized. She owed the woman so much. This job would have been much more difficult if she'd had to stop and pick up Evan each day. "Evan, you like Miss Francie a lot, don't you?"

He nodded. "Can I tell you a secret? I pretend she's my real grandma. She does cool stuff with me, and she never gets mad no matter what I do. Yesterday we walked along the creek and we found this big spot that was wide and deep, and she showed me how to skip rocks. Isn't that cool?"

"Very cool, but you know to stay away from the deep—"

"I know, Mom." Evan rolled his eyes. "Miss Francie already told me."

Gemma couldn't argue with her son's observations. Francie was the perfect grandma. Nothing like her own mother, who had little use for her grandchild. Still, a surprise party was a pretty big request. She stopped the car beside the cottage.

"Please, Mom. I want to surprise her for her birthday."

The knot that had started forming in her chest grew. But she wanted to reward Evan's thoughtfulness. "I'll think about it."

Evan huffed out a disappointed breath before getting out of the car. It wasn't the request that bothered her, it was the memories it had unearthed. It was the moment when she realized she was a disappointment to her mother.

She knew Francie wouldn't react the same way, but the memories and the emotions an event like this brought up were still painful—and once released hard to conquer again. But this wasn't about her—it was about Evan. She'd come to Dover to start fresh and the Montgomerys had opened their hearts and their doors to her and her boy. Her own reservations shouldn't matter.

Tapping lightly on her son's door, she peeked in and found him sitting on his knees in front of the window, arms resting on the sill, staring outside. She joined him, brushing aside the curtain. "It's beautiful here."

Evan nodded. "I like all the trees. They're great for climbing."

"I've been thinking about your idea, and if you really want to, we can give Miss Francie a surprise birthday party. But you have to help."

Evan jumped up and wrapped his arms around her waist. "Thanks, Mom. I'll help. I promise. When can we start? What do we do first—call people or should I make her a present?"

"Slow down, kiddo. Let's go make a list. Then we'll have to check with Mr. Linc to see if it's okay."

Evan dashed out into the other room; Gemma followed. Whatever bad memories this party might churn up, it would be worth it to see her son so happy. But what would Linc think of their request? Would he get on board or would he challenge every detail the way he did her Christmas events? She dismissed the thought. The only one she was concerned about pleasing was Evan.

The thought had barely formed when she realized it was a lie.

Wednesday evening, Linc darted behind Gemma's cottage and onto the back porch. He didn't want his mother to see him going inside and ruin the surprise. He tapped on the door, peering through the panes. Gemma stood at the counter. She turned and looked at him and his heart made a loud thump inside his chest. He stepped inside, wrapped in the enticing aroma of warm cake and fresh coffee. One look at Gemma wiped everything from his mind. Her green eyes were shadowed and dull, her lips pressed tightly together, and he suspected she was on the verge of tears. He approached her cautiously. "How's it going?"

Gemma shrugged. "Fine. Awful." She shook her head, sending her wavy hair floating around her shoulders. "I just need to make sure everything is perfect."

Linc studied her more closely, trying to understand. "It'll be okay. There's no prize for perfection."

Gemma suddenly pressed her fingertips to her lips. Her shoulders sagged and she bent forward slightly. She glanced over her shoulder at him, and the fear in her eyes tore at his heart. "Gemma, what's wrong?" He went to her side, leaning against the counter, resisting the urge to hold her. He'd never seen her so distressed.

She sucked in a short breath. "I have too much to do. It won't be ready and the party starts in half an hour. This was a big mistake. What if Evan has his heart broken the way I did?"

Linc laid his hand on hers. "What's this about? You're the woman who is single-handedly changing our entire Christmas. A simple birthday party for my mom shouldn't throw you a curve." Instead of his words encouraging her, they triggered a flood of tears. He guided her to the kitchen table, easing her down into the chair. He pulled another up close. "Gemma? Talk to me."

"I should never have agreed to this, but I didn't want Evan to be disappointed. I just hadn't expected to feel so…" She glanced around the room as if looking for the right word. "So terrified."

"Terrified of what?"

"That your mom won't like the party. That Evan will be crushed, and that it will all turn out badly."

Linc took her hand in his. She was shaking. "Gemma, my mom will love the party. Especially since it was Evan's idea. Why would you think differently?"

Gemma grasped his hand a little tighter, as if drawing strength from his touch. He wanted to fix this for her somehow.

"I planned a surprise party for my mom when I was eight. The cook helped me make cupcakes with blue frosting. Blue was my mother's favorite color." She sniffed and wiped tears from her cheeks. "I spent hours designing place cards and streamers, I gathered up odds and ends to decorate the table. But when my mother saw what I had done, she was horrified. I tried to tell her I'd made everything special for her, but she only scolded me for wasting her time on such useless junk. That it would have been better if I'd spent the time studying."

Linc's heart was breaking. He could see the little girl hurt in her eyes, and the pain it had caused her over the years. He couldn't begin to understand a mother who would dismiss the loving efforts of her child. His parents had both been proud of all their children's accomplishments. He stood and pulled her up with him and into a comforting embrace. His gesture released a fresh wave of tears.

"We'll cancel the party, Gemma. You're too upset. Mom will never know."

She shook her head, pulling back from his arms and wiping wetness from her cheeks. "No. Evan would be devastated. I can't do that to him. I just have to get myself together."

Linc brushed a few strands of hair from her face, wishing she would let him hold her again. "Gemma, Mom isn't critical or picky. She'll love the party no matter how it turns out. She's more interested in the thought behind things. Like bringing a pie to a new tenant, that kind of thing." He hadn't meant the comment to be funny, but it brought a light to her eyes and a small smile to her lips.

"I know you're right. I love your mom. I know she'll be happy. I guess I let the past get the better of me. I'm sorry."

"Don't be. I'm glad I was here to help. Do you want me to stay and help you finish up?"

"No. All that's left to do is set the table."

"Where's Evan?"

"He's in his room finishing his present for your mom. I'm sure he'd love to see you."

"I'll check in with him, and then I'll be back for the big surprise."

"Oh, how are you going to get her here? What about the cars parked outside? She'll see them and wonder why Seth is here."

"That's why I came in the first place. Seth will park his truck behind the cottage. Tell your friend to do the same. Text me when you're ready and I'll make an excuse to leave the house. As soon as I get here you can call her to come help with something."

"Okay." She looked like a sad little girl, and he wanted to wrap her up in his arms again, but given the way his pulse raced each time she was close, that wasn't a smart idea.

"Thanks, Linc. Sorry I fell apart."

Linc tapped her chin lightly. "No problem. That's what friends are for." He made his way down the hall to the back bedroom. He did want to see Evan, but mainly he wanted to hang around for a while to make sure Gemma was okay. He'd never seen her so vulnerable, and it left an unfamiliar ache in his chest. He might not agree with her plans to change everything, but he'd come to appreciate her optimistic outlook. Seeing her so insecure and frightened concerned him. What had happened to make her that way? It had to be more than a failed birthday party as a child.

He'd been filled with an overwhelming need to protect her and make sure she never felt inferior again. How he could accomplish that, however, was a mystery.

Chapter Seven

Happy chatter from the party in the living room followed Gemma into the kitchen as she placed the stack
of used dessert plates on the counter. Closing her eyes,
she leaned against the counter, releasing a sigh as the
last threads of tension drained from her body. The party
was winding down and none of her fears had material-
ized. In fact, everything had gone as planned. Why had
she ever doubted?

Francie had been genuinely surprised and delighted
with the party and especially appreciative of Evan. He'd
made her a gift of leaves they had collected together on
their walks in the woods and pasted on colored paper,
outlined with glitter and tiny acorns they'd gathered.
Francie had been moved to tears and placed the gift on
the mantel for everyone to see.

The only uncomfortable aspect had been Linc. He'd
kept a close eye on her. She'd been both touched at his
concern and grateful that he hadn't voiced it to her. In
fact, he hadn't spoken to her much at all. He seemed content to stand on the sidelines offering his silent support.

"You outdid yourself again." Caroline carried a tray
full of cups and glasses and set them on the counter.

"That was a great party. No one is ready to leave even though we gobbled up all the goodies."

Gemma smiled, enjoying the sense of lightness and peace that had eluded her for the past few days. "It was nice, wasn't it?"

"Francie is beaming and she's gushed over Evan. The little guy is floating on air."

"I'm so grateful. I couldn't have handled it if Francie had been upset."

Caroline faced her. "Francie is not your mother."

"I know." She scraped the plates and set them in the sink. "The Montgomerys are special. I've never known a family like them."

"One in particular."

"What are you talking about?"

"Linc—he couldn't take his eyes off you all through the party. I think he likes you. A lot."

Gemma wiped her hands on a towel. "Oh, no, that's because he stopped by earlier when I was stressing and he let me vent. We're just friends."

"Really? I thought you two were at odds over the Christmas events."

"We are, but he doesn't fight me anymore. He just doesn't like what I'm doing."

Caroline smiled and bobbed her eyebrows. "So you're starting to like the guy, huh?"

"No. Well…" How *did* she feel about Linc? "I don't hate him. He's been wonderful to Evan, and he's not cold and arrogant like I first thought. He's reserved and very intuitive." Curiosity widened her friend's eyes. Oh, no. She did not want to try to explain the way Linc always seemed to know what she's thinking. He couldn't, of course, but that was the way she felt when she found him looking at her.

"That's interesting. I used to think he was all male arrogance and pride. But after today, I think he's kind of nice. Handsome, too." Caroline fluffed her hair and struck a pose. "Now that I'm single, maybe I'll make a play for him myself."

The idea of Caroline and Linc dating sent a shot of heat through her veins. She was not jealous. She wasn't. Scooping up a candy dish, she rinsed it and changed the subject. "You never told me why you broke off with Vince. I thought he met all the qualifications on your list."

"He did, mostly." Caroline put the cap on the cola bottle and placed it in the fridge. "Vince is nice, but he's a little too laid-back. I want someone with ambition and drive."

"I thought he owned a computer graphics company."

"He does. Honestly, it's the football thing I can't deal with. He's crazy about that dumb game. He even has season tickets to the Saints games and he wants me to go with him."

Puzzled, Gemma stopped rinsing glasses and studied her friend. "But didn't he agree to go to the ballet with you?"

Caroline glared. "Whose side are you on?"

"Yours. But don't you think you're being a little picky and unfair?"

"I will not compromise on my list." She ticked off the points on her fingers. "He has to have a good job, good looks, a Christian, funny, athletic and he has to enjoy cooking, travel and the theater."

Gemma giggled. "So you want to date yourself?"

Caroline rolled her eyes. "At least I'm out there trying. It wouldn't hurt you to take a closer look at your expectations."

"What does that mean?"

"I know you've been through a lot, and it's hard for you to trust people, but that's in the past. You can't use that as an excuse to never love anyone again. There are a lot of nice guys out there. None of them are perfect, but neither are you."

"Gee, thanks."

"You know what I mean. Don't close yourself off to someone who could make you happy because you're waiting for him to let you down."

"Mom. Miss Francie is leaving," Evan said, interrupting Caroline's speech.

Gemma hurried to the living room, receiving hugs and compliments from a beaming Francie. Seth gave her a high five and shook Evan's hand, thanking them for the party. Francie carried the leaf art in her hands as if it was made of glass, promising Evan she'd put it in a place of honor. He asked if he could help and scurried out the door behind her.

Linc was the last to leave. He stopped in the doorway, holding her gaze a moment longer than necessary. Each time he looked at her she sensed the tether between them growing stronger. The idea sent a shiver along her spine. She didn't want to be connected to any man.

"Mom loved the party. Thank you for making her happy."

"You need to thank Evan. It was his idea."

"I did, but you made it happen. You're good at this, Gemma. You make things special."

She tilted her head. She hadn't expected a compliment. "Like Christmas events?"

"No comment." He smiled, then walked across the porch and down the steps.

Gemma returned to the kitchen to find Caroline had finished cleaning up and was preparing to leave.

"Super party, girlfriend. I *will* hire you to plan my wedding when the time comes." Caroline stepped onto the porch. Gemma glanced past her and saw Linc coming back across the lawn.

"Looks as though Mr. Linc wasn't ready for the party to end."

Gemma grimaced. "Don't be ridiculous. He probably just forgot something."

"Uh-huh. Like more time with you."

Before she could respond, her friend chuckled and hurried to her car, waving at Linc on the way.

Gemma swallowed past the lump in her throat. What was it about Linc that always tied her in knots? Watching him walk toward her, his broad shoulders arching side to side as he moved, the long legs eating up the ground, filled her with a confusing mixture of anticipation and dread. If she could put a name to these feelings then maybe she could start to master her reactions. Yes he was good-looking, but more than that he was compelling, and at times intimidating, but she found gentleness beyond the facade that she couldn't ignore.

She wrapped her arm around one of the porch posts. "I don't have any more cake to give you." He smiled, and the sudden weakness in her knees made her grateful for the wooden support.

Linc placed a hand on his flat belly. "No, thanks. Two pieces has done enough damage. I have an invitation for you."

He stopped at the foot of the porch steps looking up at her, and for a moment she felt like Juliet on her balcony gazing down at Romeo. Okay, it was only four little porch steps, but the Romeo part was accurate. From this level she could see the waves in his dark hair, and the thick black lashes that any women would envy. She cleared her throat of the sudden dryness.

"Mom would like you and Evan to join us for Thanksgiving dinner."

Not what she'd expected. "Oh. That's very nice, but I wouldn't dream of intruding on your family time."

"She thought you would say that, and she told me to tell you that as friends living in the cottage, that qualifies you as family."

A warm rush of affection made her smile. She could easily imagine Francie saying that. "Are you sure?"

Linc nodded, his blue eyes looking deep into hers. "The truth is there won't be much family this year. Tori is staying in California. Bethany starts rehearsals for a new show the week before Thanksgiving and Gil's tied up in Mobile. That just leaves Seth, me and Mom. We're used to having a full table, so you'd be doing us a favor."

"Sort of like stand-ins for your siblings?" She stifled a grin at the chagrined look on his face.

"No, I didn't mean it that way."

Gemma chuckled at his discomfort. He was always so controlled it was fun to shake him up. "All right. We'd be happy to accept your invitation. Evan will love it. I expect him to move his belongings into the main house any day now so he can be closer to Francie. He loves her."

"The feeling is mutual. Evan has been a blessing to my mom. Having him around has given her something to focus on instead of Dad being gone."

"Well, Evan needs her, too. So what do I need to bring? And should we dress up or is it a casual dinner?"

Linc came up the steps to stand beside her. "Church clothes are fine. But Mom usually goes all out. The good china, fancy tablecloth and silver. Flowers on the table, the whole nine yards."

Something in his attitude brought a sudden realization. "It's your favorite holiday, isn't it?"

"I guess it is. I like having everyone together around the table. Christmas is great, but it's hectic. Thanksgiving is family time."

"Well, thank your mother again for inviting us."

Linc looked at her, his gaze probing and searching, warming her blood and interrupting her heart rate.

"I will. I'm glad you agreed to come."

Gemma sensed another meaning in his tone. A personal note. Was he glad that she would be there for his favorite holiday? What did that mean? Uncomfortable with his scrutiny, she lowered her eyes.

He started down the steps, then looked back. "I told you everything would work out. With the party, I mean."

"Yes, you did. Thanks."

"Any time."

Gemma watched Linc until he disappeared into the main house. No matter how hard she tried, she couldn't keep her original opinion of Linc firmly in place. She was coming to see he was a man of deep emotions, a man who loved his family and grieved the loss of his father. He also had a caring heart.

The only aspect of Linc that she couldn't dismiss was his obvious need to be in charge and control those around him. It might be because he was the eldest and he took his responsibility to work and family seriously. But it could also mean his controlling streak was a part of his inherent personality—and was something to beware of. Time would tell.

Her cell phone rang as she was putting the last plate in the dishwasher. She glanced at the screen, bending forward and rubbing her temples. Her mother. Buoyed with the success of the party, she steeled herself and answered.

"Gemma, I haven't heard from you in months. Are you still working at that electrical business? I hate to see you wasting your talents in an insignificant business in Mississippi. You have so much more to offer," her mother said without so much as a hello.

Like touching a hot stove, old reactions kicked in. The sense of failure, the insecurities, the shame. She should never have answered the call. "No, Mother, I'm not working there anymore. I've taken a job with the local Chamber of Commerce. I'm in charge of their Christmas events." Gemma braced for the scolding. The only thing worse than not being a successful accountant would be working events again. The long silence on the other end of the call pulled the knot in her stomach tighter.

"I see. Well, obviously your recent failures haven't shown you that you're on the wrong path. I guess it'll take an even bigger fiasco to convince you that throwing parties for children and adults who would rather have a good time than better themselves isn't a valid profession."

Gemma fought back the tears. "I'm using the gifts God has given me, Mother. I'm sorry if that's not good enough for you, but it's good enough for me."

"That's the trouble, Gemma. You always had poor judgment."

"Obviously we see things differently, Mother. I have to go."

Gemma quickly ended the call. But her mother's words lay like a shroud over her mood the rest of the evening, churning up a storm of doubt and recriminations. She hated that she couldn't shake it off and let it go, but once the uncertainties bubbled up, it took a lot of prayer and self-determination to conquer them. One thing she was sure of was she was doing what she was called to do. She also knew the Montgomerys were a blessing she desperately needed. They were giving her a foundation on which to build her new life. Giving her hope that with the Lord's help she could be the kind of parent Evan needed. She didn't want her son to ever think he'd disappointed her or that something he did wasn't up to her standards.

Linc closed the hymnal and slid it back into the holder as he sat down in the pew. He'd looked forward to being in church this morning. He needed clarity and strength to get through the week ahead. He'd been struggling since the call had come in late Friday afternoon. The Coleman project had been won by their largest competitor. He couldn't remember the last time Montgomery Electrical had lost a job this size. What the loss of this job might mean to the business financially had tied a knot in his gut that he couldn't shake and raised doubts about his abilities to run the company.

He knew he needed to turn the pain and grief over to the Lord, but that was one area where he struggled. Each morning he looked to the scriptures and symbolically handed his life over to the Lord. But by the time he cranked his truck to go to work, he'd taken it all back.

He darted a quick glance at Gemma, thankful she was sitting at the other end of the pew next to his mother this morning. He had enough on his mind without being distracted by her heady jasmine scent and the shimmer of her red-gold hair. The delicate lace blouse she wore set off her green eyes and added to her femininity.

Reverend Barrett began his sermon, and Linc listened intently for a word that would soothe his troubled spirit. His concentration wavered as his problems pushed to the forefront again. He loved this church and the town he'd grown up in, but he could no longer ignore the problems Dover faced. It needed more money to flow into its economy. They were trying to regroup after the Southways closure by expanding the Christmas celebrations.

He still didn't like the changes being made, but he could acknowledge that the owners need to find ways to increase business. Though he doubted luring visitors to Dover would help his construction company much, he was now in a similar position. He'd have to beat the bushes for new projects, work around the clock if necessary. Montgomery Electrical had been in business three generations, and he wasn't about to let it end with him at the controls. He had to tell Gil, but he would hold off telling his mom for the time being until he saw how the loss would affect the bottom line.

He gave up trying to concentrate on the sermon. He'd drive out to his property later and spend some time alone with the Lord. It was easier to think there.

Linc exited the church behind his mother, Gemma and Evan. He smiled as Gemma stopped to greet several members. Her work with the Chamber had connected her with many residents beyond the store owners. Everyone liked her. He could understand why. She was warm, caring, like a sweet spring breeze.

Seth tapped his shoulder. "Can I ride home with you? We need to talk."

Linc studied his younger brother. It was obvious something was bothering him. He'd been restless all through the service. "Sure."

Inside the cab of his truck, Seth remained silent. Linc gave him time to sort out what he wanted to say. But when they neared home Linc glanced over at him. "Should I keep going?" Seth nodded. They'd driven nearly half an hour before Seth finally opened up.

"I'm leaving."

Linc gripped the steering wheel, hoping he'd heard wrong. "Where are you going?"

"Houston. I've been accepted to the police academy there. It's something I've wanted to do for a long time. I just didn't know how to tell Dad. Or Mom."

Linc fought to keep his tone calm and understanding, even as his heart cried out in protest. Another sibling was pulling away, cutting ties with the family business and striking out in a new direction. "I thought you were happy at the shop. You always seemed to like the work."

"I do. I did. But since Dad died I've been thinking about how short life is, and I don't want to wake up one day and regret that I didn't follow my dream. You know?"

Linc nodded, even though he didn't understand. He'd followed his dream. The only one he'd ever had—to run Montgomery Electrical alongside his dad. He'd lived his dream for the past decade, but now he was running things alone—without either of his brothers to shore him up.

"When?" The tightness in his throat made it hard to speak.

"The Saturday after Thanksgiving."

"Mom's going to be upset."

"A little, but I have been hinting to her a lot lately. She's always known what I really wanted to do."

"Does this have anything to do with that year you moved away? When you and Dad were fighting?"

"No. Nothing."

Blindsided again. Linc resisted the urge to pound the steering wheel with a fist. He'd had no idea Seth wanted another career. He'd foolishly assumed that everyone loved the family business as much as he did. His sisters, he could understand. But Seth? He prayed Gil wouldn't suddenly resign, as well.

"Are you mad?"

Linc stole a glance at his younger brother. Hurt. Wounded. Shocked. "No. Surprised."

"I know the timing stinks, but I think this is what the Lord wants me to do, Linc."

How could he argue with that? "Okay. But you hear me. You'd better be the best cop they've ever had or I'll come to Texas and ream you a good one."

Seth laughed. "You sound just like Dad."

Linc's heart tightened. No, he could never sound like Dad. Pulling into the next driveway, he turned the truck around and headed back home. Wondering if the bad news would ever stop rolling into his life.

Gemma stepped onto the front porch, inhaling the earthy fall air deep into her lungs. The Sunday-afternoon sun was bright and warm. The chill of the past few days had been replaced with balmy weather, inviting her outside to enjoy the beautiful day the Lord had created. Francie had taken Evan to the movies right after church, leaving Gemma with an afternoon all to herself. Finally she had time to start the book she'd bought weeks ago.

She glanced up when she heard Linc's truck coming down the driveway. Church had ended an hour ago. Curious, she watched the brothers emerge from the red Chevy. Seth went directly inside. Linc lagged behind, one hand resting on the truck roof, the other set on his hip. She knew the pose. Something was bothering him.

Predictably, he glanced over at her. The crease in his forehead revealed his troubled mood. She waved and he headed in her direction. He walked like a man with a burden. His usually squared shoulders were curved forward, and his stride was slow and reluctant. She hoped nothing bad had happened. The Montgomerys had been through enough.

"Is everything all right? Did you and your brother have a disagreement?"

Linc stepped onto the porch, leaning one shoulder against the post, slipping a hand into the front pocket of his dress slacks. "No. Not exactly." He shook his head slowly, as if struggling to grasp what had happened. "He's leaving. He's going to the police academy in Houston."

No wonder Linc was stunned. "That's a big life change. Has he always wanted to go into law enforcement?"

"Apparently. I know he's always admired cops, but I never figured he'd leave the company."

"Are you angry?"

"No." He rubbed his forehead. "I'm shocked. Confused. Another sibling is walking away from the family when we need each other most."

"He's not walking away, Linc. He just wants to live his life his way."

"But why now? We just lost our dad. We should be drawing closer, standing together."

Gemma resisted the urge to give him a hug. "I can't imagine how you must feel or what your family is going through, but everyone has to follow their own dreams. I don't think that means they are rejecting you or your family."

"We're coming into the most important family time of the year. Do you have any idea how many traditions our family has? They'll mean even more this year. But not if no one is here to share them."

"Maybe it's time to start new traditions."

Linc set his jaw. "What do you have against tradition, Gemma? Why are you so determined to change everything?"

"I don't have anything against tradition. I just never had any."

His expression shifted from puzzlement to one of determination. "I'd like to show you something. Will you take a ride with me?"

"All right."

Linc was silent as they rode. He steered the vehicle past the garage behind the main house and along a dirt road that led into the pines. She stole a glance at him, but his rigid jaw and stiff shoulders suggested he wasn't ready to talk. She'd wanted to be understanding about Seth leaving, and about his concerns regarding his family, but she had no reference points to draw from. Family and traditions had no significance in her world.

Someone had once asked her why she liked planning events. She'd had no answer at the time, but she'd come to understand that she liked making events special and memorable for others because she had none of her own to cherish.

Linc made a slow turn onto another dirt road that wound beneath massive live oaks and down a gentle slope. As they broke through the trees a lovely stream came into view and off to one side, an old boarded-up farmhouse. The scene was so picturesque she wished she'd brought her pad and pencil so she could sketch it to enjoy later. She'd have to settle for a few pictures on her cell phone.

Pulling to a stop, Linc stared straight ahead for a long moment, before getting out and coming to open her door. "Where are we?"

"My land."

"It's beautiful." The air was thick with the scent of pine and autumn.

Linc strolled slowly toward the stream bank. "This was the first piece of land my great-grandfather purchased when he came south. He built the old farmhouse and lived here most of his life. He started buying up more land around it, and eventually owned a couple thousand acres. But when my grandfather grew up he didn't want to farm. He'd learned electrical work in the service and decided to start his own company."

"Did you inherit the land?"

"Dad gave us each acreage when we turned twenty-one. I chose this piece because of the tradition. It's been passed down to the eldest son for generations."

Gemma saw the pride in his blue eyes and heard the reverence in his tone. She resisted the urge to reach out and take his hand. "What do you plan to do with it?"

"Build a home for my family. Right here." He gestured to the spot on which they were standing. "Beside the stream under these old oaks."

"And the old house. Can it be restored?"

"I'd always hoped so. I've tried to keep it sealed up against the elements, but a friend of mine looked at it and said it's not worth saving. I guess I'll try to salvage what I can to use in a new house someday."

She stared at his strong profile. Sensing his deep love for the place on which he stood. His vulnerability touched her heart. Never would she have expected him to have a deep sentimental streak or such devotion to his heritage. Linc had roots, purpose and a past that defined him. What would it be like to belong to a family with ties stretching back generations? Her own grandparents were gone, and she'd barely known them. Family gatherings and holiday celebrations weren't things the Butlers gave more than a passing nod to.

"I think I'm beginning to understand your definition of *tradition*. I'm glad you brought me here."

Linc looked her in the eyes, a small smile on his lips.

"I've never shown anyone outside the family this place before."

The vulnerability she saw in his expressive eyes, tugged at her heart. "I'm honored. Truly. It's a beautiful location. It would be a lovely family estate."

"I've had plenty of offers to buy it. But I'll never sell."

"I can't blame you. Living here would be wonderful." She slipped her hand in his and he squeezed it gently. Her breath caught at the look in Linc's eyes. There was a softness, a longing, as if he'd pulled back a curtain and allowed her to see something deeply personal. Slowly he raised his free hand, resting it against the side of her face. Against her will she leaned into his palm, his warmth flowing into her senses.

"I wanted you to understand."

"Why?" Did he want her to care? To back down?

His cell phone beeped, shattering the moment. She looked away, gathering her senses. When she turned back, Linc had reverted to his cool, controlled self.

"I should get you back. Mom and Evan are home."

Disappointment weighed down her mood. She wanted to stay here and explore, to walk under the gnarled oaks and follow the riverbank. She wanted to go inside the old house and discover its secrets. Maybe she'd ask Linc to bring her back.

Linc took her hand again as they walked slowly back to the truck. Gemma studied him as they drove home. Seeing Linc so vulnerable and honest had shifted something deep inside, forcing her to acknowledge that her attraction to him was growing and deepening every day. More troubling was the fact that she wanted him to feel the same way. She wanted him to care about her as more than just a friend. The thought sent a jolt through her system. It had been years since she'd wanted a man's attention, and that scared her more than anything had in a very long time.

What if she made another mistake? What if Linc wasn't all he appeared to be?

No. She'd better douse this attraction with a bucket of common sense and keep her focus on the only things that really mattered: Evan and the Christmas events.

Linc looked over at her and smiled. Common sense vanished like morning mist in sunlight.

She was in big trouble. Big, big trouble.

Chapter Eight

Gemma fastened one side of her hair back with a barrette, then did the same on the other side. She'd considered a different hairstyle, but her nerves were on edge, and she'd opted for simple and easy instead. She hadn't spoken to Linc since the day he'd taken her to see his property. She'd caught a glimpse of him as he was leaving for work one morning and waved, but he either hadn't see her or was ignoring her.

Was he was regretting telling her about his plans for his land? He'd admitted he'd never brought anyone there before. If he was worried she'd share the information with someone else, he shouldn't. She understood the importance of trust. She wanted to assure him of that, but his absence over the past few days suggested he wanted to forget the whole thing. Whatever the cause behind his standoffish behavior, it worked to her advantage, helping her get control of her runaway attraction. Any hurt feelings she might harbor were her own fault.

Evan stepped into her bedroom, his mouth pulled downward in an unhappy frown. "Is this okay?"

Gemma scanned his new jeans and the long-sleeved

red polo shirt he usually wore to church. "That's fine, sweetheart."

"I still don't see why I can't wear my flag football shirt."

"Because it's a holiday and Coach said his family dresses up for Thanksgiving." She doubted Francie would turn Evan away even if he wore his pajamas to dinner. Evan shuffled away and Gemma checked her appearance one last time. She'd settled on a long burgundy skirt, cream-colored knit top with ruched sleeves and had added a chunky necklace in fall hues with matching earrings. It was one of her favorite and most comfortable outfits and she wanted to feel at ease today. Gemma adjusted her necklace and took a deep breath. Her stomach swirled with a mixture of excitement and dread. Thanksgiving dinners past had always been stressful and ended in a huge argument when things didn't go the way her mother planned. She knew now the Montgomerys weren't like that, but she couldn't keep the anxiety from jangling her nerves.

Francie met them at the front door. Evan went immediately into her arms for a hug. Gemma noticed that she was dressed in jeans and a sweater. Definitely not church clothes. Stepping into the foyer, her senses were engulfed in the welcoming aroma of turkey and trimmings. Her anxiety vanished. She'd come to know Francie Montgomery well over the past month. She had no reason to be concerned.

Linc appeared and came toward them. Her pulse raced at the sight of him. He wore khaki trousers and a long-sleeved dark blue polo shirt that matched his eyes. He looked absurdly handsome, but the crease between his eyes and the rigid set to his jaw told her something had upset him. He tried to disguise it with a smile and a show of affection toward Evan, but failed miserably.

Francie motioned them toward the dining room. "Everything is ready. We can eat at any time." She walked off with Evan.

Gemma looked at Linc. "Is everything okay?"

He nodded, running a hand down the back of his neck. "Yes. Maybe. I don't know."

Her concern swelled. Linc was never indecisive. "If you'd like us to leave... I mean, if this isn't a good time we can—"

"No. I'm glad you're here. You're the only familiar thing here at the moment."

"I don't understand." Linc took her hand and walked into the formal dining room, stopping in the archway. "Look."

She scanned the place mats on the table, the food spread out on the buffet, plates, silverware and glasses stacked at one end of the expansive formal table. "It looks nice."

"No. It's all wrong. It's a buffet, not a dinner."

Now she understood. She remembered what he'd said about the family traditions—china, silver, flowers. Gemma studied Linc's expression. He looked like a disappointed and confused little boy. "I see what you mean. Did you ask your mom why she changed things?"

"I did. She said the same thing she says all the time now. She didn't feel like going to all that trouble."

She laid her free hand on his arm, eager to soothe his worry. "I can understand that. It must be hard to do things the same when the most important person in her life is gone."

Linc shook his head, his blue eyes seeking her understanding. "No. Keeping things the same *is* the comfort. That's why tradition is so important."

Gemma started to respond, but Seth entered the room with a basket of hot rolls, followed by Francie with the ice bucket. Evan brought up the rear.

Francie waved her hand toward the buffet. "Dig in while everything is hot. Linc, would you say the blessing, dear?"

Linc muttered a short prayer, and the confusion and sadness in his voice made Gemma long to put her arms around him. Today was his favorite holiday and it wasn't going the way he'd hoped. It was a feeling she knew well. So many things he'd counted on were changing. Like the Christmas celebrations.

Francie and Evan filled their plates from the spread on the buffet. Gemma followed, acutely aware of Linc behind her, speaking quietly with his brother Seth.

Seated at the table, Gemma watched the family interact, her heart weighing heavily inside her chest. The absence of Dale Montgomery was a palpable presence in the room. They were all trying to push through the sadness, but obviously each was struggling. Francie paid a lot of attention to Evan, telling him stories and asking him about school and the football team. Seth seemed quiet, not like his usual gregarious self. Something was wrong. Something more than missing Mr. Dale.

The meal was delicious no matter how it was served. When Francie excused herself to get the dessert, Seth went to help his mother and Linc stood and walked into the other room. Gemma rose and followed him into the formal living room. He stood in front of the window, shoulders rolled forward, arms wrapped around his torso. She wanted to place her hand between his shoulder blades and rub the tension from his back.

He turned and smiled at her. "Did you get enough to eat?"

"Yes. Too much. Your mother is a wonderful cook."

"She is. The best."

"So what's wrong? Is it because she changed the dinner to a buffet?"

Linc eyes narrowed. He set his hands on his hips. "No."

"You don't lie very well."

He rubbed his forehead. "Yeah, all right. That's part of it. Seth told Mom he's leaving."

"Oh, Linc. How did she take it?"

"As if it was no big deal. I don't think she cares. She doesn't seem to care about anything anymore."

She ran her hand lightly over his back, keenly aware of the strength and warmth beneath her fingers. "Linc, she's grieving the loss of her husband. That's not something you get over quickly. What did you expect her to do?"

He shrugged. "Order him to stay. Tell him to wait until next year. Her family is leaving her all alone."

"She has you. And us."

Linc reached out and fingered a strand of hair that was resting across her shoulder. His fingers grazed her neck, releasing a flood of warmth in her veins. His eyes softened, a small smile lifting one side of his mouth.

"That's true. I didn't think it was a good idea at first for her to watch Evan. I thought it would be too much for her, but he makes her happy. I'm glad he's here. And you."

There was an intimate tone in his voice that caught her breath. "I'm glad, too. You all are showing me the way a loving family is supposed to be. I've never known a loving home like yours."

Seth called from the dining room, "If you want any dessert you'd better get in here before I eat it all."

Gemma and Linc returned to the dining room, where Francie was handing out plates of pecan pie. Seth accepted his plate and gave her a kiss before sitting down. She smiled, but it never reached her eyes. Linc was wrong. Francie cared very much about Seth leaving. But she wouldn't ask him to stay. She knew Francie well enough to know that.

When the guys retreated to the living room to watch football, Gemma helped Francie clean up. "Thank you for inviting us today. The meal was delicious."

Francie smiled as she pulled open the dishwasher. "That's good to hear. I was afraid it would all taste like sawdust. So much of cooking is the love you put into it as you prepare. Without that important ingredient it's just food. My heart wasn't into the meal this year, or anything else, for that matter."

"That's understandable."

Evan ran back into the room, holding his football. He carried it with him everywhere. "We're going outside to play. Bye."

Seth ambled through, lifting a piece of turkey from the platter on his way. Linc sauntered into the kitchen. He'd changed into worn jeans and a long-sleeved T-shirt with Mississippi State on the front.

Francie motioned to Gemma. "Go. Watch them play. I'll be right out."

Gemma didn't argue. She slipped out onto the front porch and took a seat in one of the cushioned chairs. Linc and Evan teamed up against Seth. The brothers shouted and laughed and treated her son as if he were one of the big guys, making sure he scored his share of touchdowns, but not sparing him when it came time to tackle. Thankfully, their brand of tackling consisted of scooping Evan up and running with him. The scene filled her with a sweet lightness.

Francie joined her on the porch. "I used to play with them—the whole family got into the game. Linc and his dad would team up against Gil and Seth. Each team took one of the girls. I miss that. How about you? Any siblings?"

"An older sister, but we weren't close. Our family wasn't big on holidays."

"Then, you must be enjoying being part of the Dover Christmas?"

"I am. Thank you again for today. I can't remember a more relaxing day."

"I'm glad, dear. We've enjoyed having you. You and Evan have a special place in my heart."

Gemma looked away, not wanting her friend to see the moisture forming in her eyes. This was the way she'd envisioned family to be. Loving, supportive and devoted. A shout brought her attention to Linc. The crease in his forehead was gone, replaced with a wide smile as he tossed the ball to Evan. Seth caught it instead. She laughed as Seth spun, ducked and avoided Evan and Linc and raced to the magnolia tree goal line.

Linc and Evan hung their heads, hands on hips, mirroring each other. She smiled, clasping her hands in front of her chin. Evan adored Linc. The way a boy would his father.

A cell phone chirped. Francie pulled her phone from her pocket and answered, then muttered a soft exclamation of surprise.

Gemma glanced at her friend, her blood chilling at the look of shock on Francie's face. "What is it? Is everything all right?"

Francie shook her head and called to her eldest son.

Linc tossed the ball to Evan and trotted over to them. "What's going on? Mom, you okay?"

"Pete McCorkle called. Leon Skelton, the Chamber treasurer, was arrested in Vicksburg this afternoon for embezzlement of Chamber funds."

"What? How much of the money did he take?"

Francie gripped the phone tightly in her hand. "I don't know exactly, but Pete said it was significant."

Linc pulled his cell phone from his back pocket. "We should talk to the mayor, or Chief Reynolds. He'll have more information."

Gemma's heart sank. Questions swirled through her mind, mingled with shock and confusion. What would this mean to the celebrations? How could they possibly move forward with no money? Blood roared in her ears and her throat closed up as she anticipated the potential problems ahead.

All her hopes and plans were disintegrating. She couldn't fail again. Her résumé would stop with her failed business; no one would hire her. She'd have to go back to accounting. Or worse still, go back to her parents. No. She shook her head, dislodging the negative thoughts. She'd face this the way she had everything else. Dig in and find a way to make it work.

Ball game forgotten, Gemma followed Francie back inside. Seth settled Evan beside him on the sofa to watch more of the game, leaving her and Linc to join Francie in the kitchen.

"What will this mean to Dover? For the Christmas events?" Gemma knew it was a silly question, but she'd hoped that maybe it wasn't as bad as it sounded.

"I don't know, but I'll make some calls and see what I can find out."

Gemma's shock gave way to action. She needed to

make some decisions, too. If the money for the events was gone, she needed to rethink some of her plans. She wanted to be prepared to shift gears. No way was this going to prevent her from completing the job she was hired to do.

"I'd better go. I need to see what adjustments I might need to make. I think I'll give Leatha a call. She always has her ear to the ground."

Francie gave her a warm hug. "Good idea. Leave Evan here. He can finish watching the ball game with Seth."

Her gaze drifted to her son, who was seated on the edge of the sofa beside Seth, the football in his hands, engrossed in the game. She prayed her dreams of proving herself and starting over hadn't just been sacked like the quarterback on the TV screen.

Linc gave Gemma an hour before using the container of leftovers his mother had assembled as his excuse to go check on her. He hoped she'd learned more than they had about Leon's arrest. All they'd managed to find out was that Leon had also stolen money from the Dover bank where he was employed, apparently to support his gambling habit.

He looked up as Gemma opened the door, and the expression on her face told him everything he wanted to know. She was fearful and worried. It was a good thing he had the dish in his hand or he would have pulled her into his arms immediately.

"Mom sent you some leftover turkey with orders to eat something." He hadn't intended to be amusing, but his comment made her smile, lifting some of the darkness from her eyes.

"That's sweet." She took the container and stepped back. "Come on in. I need a break."

Linc's heart soared at her invitation. He followed her into the kitchen, passing the cluttered dining room table where she was working. "How's it going?"

Gemma stored the food in the fridge, then tugged her hair behind her ears. "All I know is that the money for the Christmas committee is gone. All of it. Pete has called a meeting for tomorrow night to regroup."

He swallowed, clenching his teeth. It was a rotten situation. She'd worked hard to put the Christmas events together and now it was all for nothing. Even though he'd been against the changes, Gemma didn't deserve to have her plans destroyed this way. He wished there was something he could do to make it right. "So does this mean you'll have to cancel everything?"

Gemma's smile vanished and her eyes darkened, shooting sparks in his direction. "You'd like that, wouldn't you?"

"No. Of course not, but can you go on without any money?"

"I don't know yet. I'll have to change some things, but I plan on keeping as many events as I can, so you can stop trying to control me."

"I'm not."

"Aren't you? You've been against this from the start, thinking you knew best, that your old ways were the only ways. Well, you can forget it." She crossed her arms over her chest and glared. "People have controlled me all my life, trying to make me into what they wanted, overpowering my wishes. Saying they knew what's best for me. I'm not letting you do that. And while we're on the subject, you need to stop trying to control your family or they'll start to resent you and leave permanently."

Linc stared at her, trying to figure out how things had

shifted. "I'm not trying to control them. I'm trying to keep the family together."

"Well, you won't do that by holding on the way you are."

"I didn't realize you were an expert on keeping families together." Linc regretted the words instantly when he saw how they affected her. She paled and a flash of pain darkened her eyes.

"I am. Now, if you'll excuse me, I have work to do."

"You're going forward with everything?" She wasn't giving up. Good for her.

"Yes. Whether you like it or not, Dover's Christmas *will* happen. I'm not going to fail a second time."

Linc studied her. What did she mean? "A second time?"

Gemma shook her head and lowered her head. "Nothing. Forget it."

He took a step closer. He needed to know. "What happened?"

She kept her back to him. "I had an event planning business. It failed. That's all you need to know."

Linc pulled her around to face him, absorbing the icy glare in her green eyes. She'd added another question to his list about her past. She put on a happy, confident face most of the time, but something had wounded her deeply. Something she kept hidden, and he wanted to know what it was.

"So our Christmas celebrations are your way of proving yourself?"

"Yes. There's nothing wrong with that. Success here will open doors. It'll give me the chance to start a new business or get hired by an established company in a big city."

He didn't like the sound of that. He'd grown accus-

tomed to Gemma and Evan living in the cottage. He liked
being tangled up in their lives. He wasn't sure when he'd
changed his mind about that, but the thought of them
moving on, away from Dover, hit him hard. Too hard.

"You need to go. I have work to do," she repeated.

Linc moved to the door, but he was determined to get
to bottom of Gemma's past. Understanding her, knowing her fears, was suddenly very important. Having her
in his life was suddenly paramount, too.

Friday passed in a flurry of phone calls, emails and re-
structured events. By the time Gemma left for the meeting with the Chamber and the owners that evening, she
wasn't sure she could even think straight. But somehow
she'd managed. Now she waited while the conversation in
the conference room slowly died down. She'd addressed
the situation, laid out her plans for simpler versions of
her original ideas and tried to reassure the store owners
that the Dover Christmas weekends would go forward
on schedule.

Fortunately some of the things she'd purchased had
already been paid for and delivered. The ads she'd placed
and the marketing had been taken care of, as well. But
there were still big obstacles to the weekend. Especially
the big lighting kickoff.

As the owners settled down the questions started up.
Gemma answered each one calmly, meeting every negative with a positive. Her confidence grew. This is what
she loved: creating on the fly, letting her imagination run
free and finding new inspiration.

"I know you all have concerns, but there is one area
that this financial loss will seriously impact, and that's
the lights on the storefronts. I've purchased lights for the
town to use every year, and they have been delivered,

but I couldn't pay for them. I convinced the company to hold off on returning them so we could come up with a solution.

"There's also the matter of hanging the lights and drapes over the streets. I had arranged for a professional crew to do that, but we can't afford to use them now. I'm working on some alternatives. If any of you have lights you could donate or if you could help hang the street drapes, please speak to me at the end of the meeting."

By the time the meeting concluded, Gemma was tired, but confident. Most of the owners' fears had been eased, but she still had a huge obstacle to overcome. All her ads and marketing hyped the Dover Glory Lights as the main event, the one that would ensure the success of the following weekends. If she couldn't come up with payment, the company could very well take them back. And without the lights the other events would fizzle and fail.

Tom Durrant of Durrant's Hardware approached her, a warm smile softening distinguished features. "Gemma, I've been talking to my family and the boys and I are more than willing to help hang the lights. Just let us know."

Tom had two sons and a son-in-law who lived in Dover and were always willing to help out when needed. Gemma wanted to hug the man. "Bless you. That will help a lot."

"I'll see if I can round up a few other volunteers. We're all counting on this Christmas to boost our business."

"I appreciate this so much." Gemma's spirits rose. She'd prayed the town wouldn't be discouraged by the loss of funds, but part of her had been skeptical. Now she felt ashamed of her doubt.

A middle-aged gentleman tapped her shoulder. "Ms. Butler. I'm Neal Smith. I own the upholstery shop on

Church Street. I know you have backup plans, and you've made it seem like things will be okay, but I just can't see my way clear to spend the time or the money on these schemes. I'm 'fraid you'll have to scratch me off your list."

She tried to hide her disappointment behind a confident smile. "Mr. Smith, I understand your concerns, but why don't you and I talk and see if we can find a compromise?"

"Nope. My mind's made up. I'm through with this nonsense."

Gemma watched him go, her earlier triumph wilting like a flower in a drought. She scanned the other owners making their way out of the room, wondering how many more would back away from the celebrations. Success would depend on everyone doing their part, and she'd promised the town success. It was important to them, and for her future and Evan's.

Gathering up her belongings, she made her way to her car. Voices drew her attention. Two men stood in front of a store a few doors down. Linc and Mr. Smith. They shook hands. Smith nodded, then Linc patted him on the shoulder before walking away.

Something about the conspiratorial exchange left a sick feeling in the pit of her stomach. Linc had been resistant to her changes from the start, but surely he wouldn't turn people against her. Would he? He'd been quick to assume she'd call everything off after the theft. Was he using that as leverage to get people to drop out?

She shoved the notion aside, dismissing her suspicions as nothing more than the imaginings of a fatigued mind. She headed home, focusing instead on alternatives to her Christmas light kickoff. The event was a week away and most of the decorating had to be done. It was too late to change any of the ads she'd placed. She'd looked into renting the lights for the month instead, but that had also proved far too expensive. She'd approached the mayor and he promised to speak to the city council about designating funds, but he didn't have much hope. The whole purpose of the Christmas expansion was to add to the city coffers. Not drain off more.

Gemma didn't have a solution, but she knew in her heart it would all work out. Even if she had to climb a shaky ladder and tack each string of lights in place herself. She refused to cancel the holiday celebrations. The town was counting on her, and she was counting on its success to reboot her career.

By the time she'd arrived back at the cottage, two more owners had called and withdrawn from the window-decorating contest. There were already several empty storefronts around the square. If many more owners pulled out, that would leave long stretches of darkness, which in turn would do little to draw visitors to town. Her kickoff would only work if everyone participated and every store was blazing with lights. Anything less and it would be no different from any other small town— ho-hum lights scattered haphazardly around town.

She needed a sounding board. An impartial observer. Thankfully Caroline was home when she called. She listened as Gemma expressed her concern. "What bothers me the most is why so many have suddenly decided to withdraw. The Chamber had promised only a small amount of financial help to the merchants as incentive."

"Maybe they're just demoralized that one of their own has stolen from them."

"Or they've lost faith in me." She rubbed the dull ache in her temple.

"Impossible. Maybe there's something else going on.

You don't think Linc is convincing people to back out, do you?"

Gemma closed her eyes against the heaviness sinking through her body. She didn't want to believe Linc would stoop to such a thing, but she'd seen him and Neal Smith joking together only moments after Neal had pulled out. "I don't know what to think."

"Well, I don't think Linc would ever stoop to that. And I don't think you do, either. You're just looking for an explanation and he's the likely target."

"Well, he does like to be in control."

"That's your fear talking. Linc is a good guy. Don't go throwing up walls that aren't needed. You'll regret it. I promise."

The odd tone in her friend's voice told Gemma they weren't talking about Linc any longer. "Something is bothering you. What's going on?"

"I missed Vince. More than I ever expected to. I sat down and made a list of the things I liked and the things that drove me nuts, and the list of likes was way longer. He called and wanted to try again so he's coming over this weekend to talk things through."

"Are you sure? I don't want to see you hurt."

"I am, and I have you to thank for it."

"Me? What did I do?"

Caroline chuckled softly. "I heard myself telling you that no one is perfect, and I realized that's what I've been looking for. Perfection. My list didn't allow for faults and flaws and humanness. Vince isn't perfect, but neither am I."

Gemma ended the call, thinking about what her friend had said about faults and flaws. How did you tell which ones were tolerable and which weren't? It was a subject she didn't have time to examine right now.

* * *

By Monday morning Gemma was too frustrated and too tired to think clearly. All her efforts to find lights or people to donate money toward them had come to nothing. She believed in her heart that something would turn up, but she had no idea what it would be. Mostly she wanted an explanation from Linc. Three more stores had pulled out. She wanted to believe Caroline was right about him, but the evidence was piling up.

Since there was no ball game this week, she hadn't seen Linc since he'd stopped by the cottage on Thanksgiving night. Francie told her he was working overtime, looking for someone to take Seth's place at the shop. But she planned on making him her first call when she reached the office. She needed to settle this once and for all.

As she approached the intersection of Main and Peace Streets downtown, she found the street barricaded. She parked on a side street and hurried down the sidewalk to the office. Two Montgomery Electrical bucket trucks were positioned in the middle of the block. Men in the buckets were attaching the Christmas wreath drapes in place across the street. At the end of the courthouse park, along Church Street, a fire truck with its bucket raised was doing the same. Stunned, she could only stand and watch. Who had arranged this? More important, who was paying for it?

Leatha hurried toward her from the office. "Isn't it wonderful? All this help. It's a blessing from God, and the good folks here in Dover. And the best part, the lights are all here. Paid for by an anonymous donor."

Gemma jerked around to look at her assistant. "When did that happen? No one told me."

"I don't know. Sometime over the weekend. There was

a message when I got in today saying the lights would be delivered this morning. Before I could call you, Mr. Linc showed up and hauled off the lights, then Neal Smith— he's one of our volunteer firemen—came by and asked for the plans on how to hang the lights on the storefronts. Isn't it exciting?"

Smith? The man she'd seen Linc talking to the other night. She spun around and headed toward the office, Leatha hurrying to keep up. "I need some answers."

"Well, why don't you go ask Mr. Linc? He's right up there." Letha pointed skyward to the nearest bucket truck.

Gemma tilted her head back, trailing her gaze up the extended metal arm until she saw a familiar pair of shoulders beneath a hard hat. "Linc is hanging the lights?"

Leatha nodded. "One of his employees is in the other truck."

Linc shifted position in the bucket and glanced down. Their eyes met. He smiled and offered a small wave. She raised her hand in return. She didn't know what to think. She'd spent all weekend growing more and more outraged, thinking he was sabotaging her plans when he was doing the opposite.

"Hey, Ms. Butler."

Gemma pulled her attention from Linc to the man jogging toward her. Neal Smith. He smiled, catching his breath before speaking. "I've been thinking about what I said about not wanting to be in that window thing. I just don't have any imagination, that's all. Maybe you could stop by and give me some ideas?"

Gemma swallowed the shout of joy rising up in her throat. "Of course. I can even help you decorate if you'd like."

"That would be real nice. Now that I see all the lights

and stuff going up, I'd sure hate to be the Scrooge with the dark storefront window this weekend."

Laughter escaped her throat and she clasped her hands together. She wanted to spread her arms wide and dance around the park, but first she had to find the generous person who'd paid for the lights. "Thank You, Lord. You are always faithful."

With the decorations well in hand, Gemma returned to her office, trying to figure out what had caused Linc's change of heart about the Christmas events. Maybe Caroline was right and she was too quick to think the worst. Over time it had become a habit. One that she should work to change.

The sight of Linc high in the bucket hanging lights— lights he'd been opposed to—filled her with an unusual kind of happiness. She couldn't deny her attraction to him any longer. He invaded her thoughts at night, she wondered about him during the day, and when he was near, she wanted to watch his every move. The way he walked, quick and deliberate, the way he rubbed his forehead when he was irritated or troubled. How he always stood with his weight thrust onto one hip, a masculine pose that only made him more attractive. But most important, she was beginning to think he was a man she could trust. A man who could be counted on.

It had been a long time since she'd even considered that idea. The thought tied her stomach in a knot.

Because what if she was mistaken? She'd been wrong before. Horribly wrong.

Chapter Nine

Linc secured the end of the wire to the top edge of the building, then leaned back and examined his work. The clear lights outlined the facade of the old abandoned hotel and the windows. He knew there were more lights to position on the lower level, but he couldn't make heads nor tails of Gemma's plans. Clearly her months working for Montgomery Electric hadn't taught her the proper way to lay out wiring.

Glancing downward he stared at the front door of the Chamber offices, hoping for a glimpse of Gemma. He'd expected her to be scurrying around below making sure everyone did things properly, but she'd barely acknowledged him with a halfhearted wave, then retreated into her office. Of course she hadn't known he'd be here this morning. He'd made all the arrangements without consulting her. It avoided any more confrontations. He shoved aside the thought that she might not appreciate his stepping in to fix things. He'd cross that bridge if and when he came to it.

Linc grasped the controls and lowered the bucket. Time to talk to the lady in person. Not an unpleasant prospect. She'd looked stunned to find him hanging lights. She wasn't alone in that. He'd never expected to be helping this way. After the shock of Leon's embezzlement, and in the wake of Gemma's determination to press on with the events, he'd found himself unwilling to let her dream or her hard work fail. Gemma had captivated him with her ability to accomplish things with a smile and enthusiasm. She'd quickly risen to the occasion, and even with the lack of funds, had found alternative ways to keep the events on track. She'd eased fears, boosted morale and inspired confidence. Everyone was counting on these events, and in a way, so was he. It was why he'd ensured their success, despite the cost.

Safely back on the sidewalk, Linc placed a call to Gemma, who agreed to meet him with the design layout so he could finish the hotel. The sight of her hurrying across the street made him smile. In her dark jeans and soft white sweater she exuded an energy and a grace that was a delight to watch. Though lately, everything she did delighted him.

She stopped in front of him, brushing a strand of hair from her cheek. "Show me what you're confused about." He nearly blurted out that he was confused by her. She had him viewing everything in his life differently, and his emotional circuits were so overloaded he couldn't sleep anymore. Clearing his throat, he opened the plans and pointed to the large overhanging metal canopy that jutted out from the hotel. "I have no idea where you want this string of lights."

She gave him a quick explanation, which, had he been blessed with even a dab of imagination, he could have figured out. He shrugged. "Yeah, that makes sense." He studied the adjacent building. It would be much simpler. The lights would follow the roofline and outline the arched windows across the front.

He looked at Gemma. She studied him with a concerned expression. "Something wrong?"

"Why are you so angry all the time?"

"What? I'm not angry."

"Then, why do you always have a frown on your face?" She placed her fingers on the spot above his nose between his eyes. He inhaled sharply at the warmth in her touch that radiated down to his toes.

Her eyes widened. "I'm sorry. I'm getting too personal."

He grasped her wrist, his thumb resting on her pulse point. It was racing. Her skin was warm and incredibly soft. "It's okay. You're not the first person to comment that I scowl a lot."

Her eyes locked with his and held him captive. He realized there were tiny gold flecks in her deep green eyes. The air between them hummed like an alternating current, linking them with an invisible force. She blinked, her long lashes brushing against her cheeks. When she met his gaze again her eyes glinted with warmth.

"Maybe you should do something for fun. Something that would make you smile more."

She sounded breathless, as if she'd just been kissed, or wanted to be. She pulled her hand from his grasp, leaving him with an odd empty feeling in the middle of his chest.

"So what do you usually do for fun?"

Linc tried to remember the last time he'd done anything for the pure pleasure of it. "I run in the morning."

"That's for exercise, not fun."

"I had fun coaching the boys. I think I might volunteer to coach basketball. The church has a team starting up after New Year's."

She clutched the papers to her chest. "You're good at it, and it did make you smile."

There was an appreciative twinkle in her eyes that gave him courage. "You like my smile?"

She shrugged. "It's not bad. I could stand to see more of it."

"Because you like my smile or because you want me happy?"

"Everyone should be happy. Come on. There must be something you look forward to?"

Being with you. He stopped the words from being spoken. "I used to look forward to breakfast with my dad. Every Saturday we'd go to the Magnolia Diner, sit in the last booth by the window and discuss things. Just the two of us."

"Did he do that with the others?"

"Yes. They each had their own special time and place." Linc caught a flicker of envy in her green eyes and recalled her comments about her family. Maybe she'd never known that kind of family closeness. Gemma looked at him with concern in her eyes.

"Maybe you should go to the diner and have breakfast one morning. Say goodbye. It might ease the pain a little."

"Alone? It wouldn't be the same."

"I'll go with you." She blinked as if she'd not meant to say the words out loud. "I mean…I like breakfast, that is."

He'd like nothing better than to share a morning with her. And Evan. Maybe he could start a new tradition. "How about this Saturday?"

"I can't. That's the judging of the lamppost contest. Your mom is a judge and she volunteered you to watch Evan. But I'm sure he'd love to have breakfast with you and carry on the tradition."

The implications sent Linc's pulse racing. Having a family of his own had been something he thought about, but always in the distant future. Lately he'd been thinking more and more about a settled life, something more than running Montgomery Electrical.

"The frown is back."

Linc looked into Gemma's smiling eyes. "Sorry, I guess I do have a lot on my mind. With Dad gone I have to step up and fill in."

"You're not your dad. You can't do things the way he did. You have to find your own path. Do things the way that works for you."

He tapped her chin with one finger. "That's good advice. How did you get so smart?"

"I've had to carve out my own path my whole life. Following in my parents' footsteps was never an option for me." She bit her lip, then smiled. "Thank you for hanging the lights. Does this mean you're finally behind the new celebrations?"

The light in her deep green eyes warmed his heart. He didn't want her to ever be disappointed. "I guess it does."

"Good. I'm glad we're finally on the same side."

"Me, too." He watched her walk away, wishing she would stay at his side. Always.

Settled at her desk once more, Gemma tried to focus on the Christmas events, but thoughts of Linc kept diverting her attention. She touched her wrist, the one he'd held, reliving the feel of his fingers on her skin. There was a magnetic force between them. An energy that she couldn't ignore, and it had all started when she saw him high in the bucket, hanging lights.

What had prompted him to help? It was a far cry from his earlier attitude, and while she was grateful, his change of heart left her off balance. His story about having breakfast with his dad had replayed in her thoughts, too, filling her with envy. She had no such memories.

No warm fuzzy recollections of family get-togethers or special times with her parents. In her home you stayed quiet, invisible and made sure you got As on all your schoolwork.

Leatha appeared in front of the desk, peering over the rim of her glasses. "Gemma. Have you decided what to do about the nativity?"

Shoving aside thoughts of Linc, she focused on the next problem. "I suppose I'm going to have to go back to the storage building and take another look at the old one." She'd ordered a new nativity, but with no money to pay for it, she'd had to cancel.

"I know you had your heart set on that shiny new nativity, but folks here had a deep affection for that old one. Some of them were sad to hear it wasn't being used this year."

"Let me guess. It was a tradition, right?"

"Yes, but it was more than that. Most people in Dover have probably forgotten, but the nativity was donated to the town by the Ballard family after the death of their infant son on Christmas Eve."

Gemma exhaled a sigh. "Oh, how sad."

"It was a difficult time. The Ballards were a well-loved family here. The town held a vigil for the baby for several years. The family eventually moved away, but the nativity always held a special significance at Christmas."

"I appreciate you sharing that with me. I'll take another look at the old one. Maybe we can get another year out of it."

It was late afternoon before Gemma found time to visit the storage building. She went immediately to the section she'd set aside for the items she planned to discard. The old nativity was near the front of the pile. Besides the canceled parade, her decision to order a new nativity had been another thing Linc had balked at. The twelve-piece set was faded and weather-beaten. The baby Jesus figure had a large hole in its side, hardly the image of the baby savior she wanted to present to new visitors. As she ran her fingers over the large gash, a scripture came to mind, reminding her of why He'd come to earth in the first place. Not to be a sweet baby in a manger but a man on a cross who died to redeem his children.

Hot tears stung the backs of her eyes. Maybe she'd been too quick to dismiss all traditions as pointless. Looking at the nativity now, she saw it in new light, a way to honor the memory of the child who was lost and the child who came to save the lost.

She'd fussed at Linc for not knowing the roots of the traditions he cherished. She owed him an apology. The more time she spent in Dover, the more she came to see that holding on to certain things in the past might be necessary. Remembering happy times or people who were no longer with us could be comforting. Most things in her past she'd worked hard to forget.

The nativity was dirty and faded, and making it presentable would be time-consuming, but she felt confident Leatha would know someone who could handle it.

A loud snap split the quiet air. A shudder shot down her spine, making her aware of how alone and isolated she was in the old building. Linc's warning to not come here by herself took on new meaning. She wished he was here. His steady, dependable presence always made her feel protected and special. And each time she was with him she took a step closer to the cliff called "falling in love." It was a very dangerous place to go.

But she didn't think she could turn back now. Linc was too tightly intertwined with her life and Evan's. Each day he wrapped another layer of himself around her heart.

His kindness, his consideration, his affection for her son, his fierce need to protect those he cared about... She was coming to understand that it derived from a well of love, and not a need to control as she'd first thought.

But there was a fine line between those two things, wasn't there? Or was it her fear talking? The rafters above creaked. Time to get out of here and back to work. Questions about Linc would have to wait.

Gemma shoved her hands into her pockets as she crossed the courthouse square Friday evening. The past week had been hectic, but exhilarating. The lights had gone up on the buildings, the street drapes installed, garlands hung along the wrought iron fence surrounding the courthouse park. The Dover bank had donated a giant tree for the square, their way of compensating for the mess Leon had created, and local church members had come together to decorate it. The tree and the brightly lit gazebo nearby were the crowning glory of the park. Santa had a special tent covering his throne, surrounded by fake packages and a few plastic reindeer.

Tonight was the grand lighting, and she'd promised to watch with Evan and Francie. The temperatures had fallen, making it perfect for visitors to watch the lights and stroll through town. She dodged a couple standing in the middle of the walkway as she headed to the far end of the park, every nerve in her body alive and rejoicing. Her campaign had succeeded. Dover's downtown streets were teeming with visitors. She sent up a prayer of thanks and one for the upcoming weekends. She'd come to love the small town, and her desire to succeed now went beyond wanting to do a good job. She wanted to be a part of their growth.

"When are the lights supposed to come on?"

The couple Gemma walked by were glancing around the darkened town. Only the usual streetlights illuminated the square. Gemma slowed and smiled. "In about ten minutes. Welcome to Dover. We're so glad you're visiting."

The woman smiled. "Are you the mayor?"

Gemma chuckled. "No. I'm with the Chamber of Commerce." She answered a few more questions before hurrying on. She wanted to be with Evan when the lights came on. She'd done all she could at this point. Linc had assigned one of his best men, Ike Walker, to take control of the actual throwing of the switch. He'd been invaluable in getting everything coordinated and connected so the whole downtown would burst into light at the moment the switch was thrown. All that was left for her to do was stand back and wait, and pray that everything went according to plan.

Spotting her son near the west side of the park, she waved, only to halt midmotion. Francie was there, but so was Linc. Her mood hitched up a couple more notches and her pulse skipped. She'd been so busy this week she hadn't actually talked to him in a few days. Her every minute had been taken up with organizing decorations, creating new designs on the fly and keeping her sanity. The events weren't complicated, but keeping everything on track was.

"Hey, Mom. When will the lights go on?" Evan bounced up and down, unable to contain his excitement.

"Soon." She glanced at Linc. There was an appreciative glint in his dark eyes that even the dim light couldn't hide. She took up a position beside Francie and behind her son. Linc stood behind her, so close she could feel the warmth of his body and a whiff of his woodsy aftershave. She resisted the urge to lean back against him.

Standing with the Montgomerys gave her a warm, inclusive feeling, as if she were really part of the family. For a brief second she allowed herself to imagine sharing the family dinners, watching the guys play ball in the yard, slipping an arm around Linc's waist. Heat infused her neck. She must be more tired than she'd thought.

She dipped her head to speak to Evan when "Joy to the World" suddenly blared from the speakers and the switch was thrown, bathing Dover in a flood of lights from all directions. Pressing her fingertips to her lips, she blinked away tears. It was more beautiful than she'd envisioned. The entire square was aglow, from the drapes over the streets and the store facades to the decorations in the park. The historic gazebo, Dover's cherished landmark, sparkled with twinkling lights.

"Whoa. Mom, it's awesome."

Applause and cheers erupted as the visitors delighted in the joyful transformation.

Francie clapped in Gemma's direction. "Well done. I knew you were the right person for this job."

Evan revolved slowly, taking in the lights on all sides of the square. "Can we walk around now and look at the store windows?"

"Of course." A rush of relief coursed through her, leaving her drained and feeling several years younger.

Francie and Evan started off. Linc stepped to her side. "Beautiful."

"What?" She looked at him, her heart skipping at the intimate smile on his face. Was he talking about the Christmas lights or something more personal?

"The town looks beautiful."

"Are you saying you were wrong?"

"Never. But I will admit to having a lack of imagination."

"Sounds like an apology to me."

Linc chuckled under his breath and fell into step beside her. He nodded toward the nativity as they passed by. "I'm glad you decided to put this back up."

"I took a closer look and discovered all it really needed was a little love. Baby Jesus had a broken section, but then I thought about the reason He came in the first place, and it didn't seem so unattractive then."

Gemma liked having Linc beside her as they strolled along the sidewalk. She had to work hard to remember to take notes of small things that needed to be addressed for the next day, and not concentrate solely on the tall, vibrant man at her side who made her feel warm, protected and very feminine.

By the time they'd circled the square, stopped for a cup of hot chocolate and examined all the decorated lampposts, Evan was growing tired and so was she. Tomorrow would be a full day of activities and she needed to be rested.

Francie took Evan home and Gemma expected Linc to go with them, but he lingered.

"Care for one more stroll through the park? I'm not ready to leave yet."

The crowds had thinned and only a few visitors filled the sidewalks. Gemma liked the idea of walking through the lights slowly. The crowds were a huge blessing, but made it difficult to fully appreciate the decorations. They'd dodged and weaved people every step of the way. Walking through the Christmas glory with Linc was an opportunity she didn't want to pass up. "All right."

Linc rested his hand on her lower back, steering her toward Church Street. But instead of crossing to the stores, he exited through the gates and stopped at the white carriage parked at the curb.

"How about we ride while we look? Enjoy a different view."

She'd made all the arrangements for this service, but it had never occurred to her to take advantage of it. Now she wanted nothing more than to sit with Linc in the charming carriage and ride through the shower of lights. She nodded, then took the hand he offered to help her into the carriage. He chose the backseat and spread the small blanket there across her lap. He spoke to the driver, then settled back.

They rode in silence for a few minutes before Linc took her hand in his. "You did a great job, Gemma. I never expected it to be so amazing."

"You didn't think I could pull it off?"

"I never doubted that." He made an expansive gesture with his hand. "But I wasn't prepared for the scope of this thing."

"You hung the lights. That should have given you some idea."

"It should have. But I was too focused on putting them exactly where your little chart said. And from that I couldn't tell what it was going to look like."

"You don't like following other people's plans. It messes with your control issues."

He shrugged. "Someone has to be in charge. Most people leave important things out, then it gets all screwed up. But you thought of everything. You are an amazing woman."

Gemma's heart pounded and a warm flush heated her skin. She looked into his eyes and saw affection. Did he see the same in hers? She'd been steadily losing her heart to him, in spite of her determination not to. "Does that mean you no longer think I'm ruining Dover's holiday?"

Linc rubbed his thumb across the back of her hand. "No. Not anymore. I've had a change of heart."

"Really? Why?"

He squeezed her hand a little tighter. "I've had a few setbacks at work that made me realize bringing more people into town could help all the business owners, not only the ones on the square."

"I hope it's nothing serious, at work, I mean."

"I'll handle it."

Gemma shivered at the look in his eyes. He was more troubled than he was letting on. Thinking she was chilled, he scooted closer and put an arm around her shoulder. She told herself to pull away, but she liked the feel of him close to her. He was warm and protective and too attractive for a weak woman like her to resist.

He tilted her chin upward, his blue gaze fixed on her mouth. Her lips parted and she leaned toward him. Her mind told her to stop this from happening, but her heart had other ideas. She'd wondered too long about his kiss.

His lips were cool, tender, and she melted against him, floating on the sweet sensation of his touch. He explored her mouth slowly, tenderly, yet with restrained passion. From deep inside, long-ignored emotion stirred, slipping past the thick wall she'd constructed around her heart. Feelings of belonging and connection. Things she'd searched for all her life, only to find betrayal instead. And pain.

She pushed away.

The surprise and confusion in Linc's eyes made her want to cry. She couldn't risk it. She called to the carriage driver to stop. Tossing the blanket aside, she stepped onto the sidewalk. Linc jumped down behind her, spinning her around to face him.

"I'm sorry. I didn't mean to upset you. I've wanted to

do that for a long time, Gemma. You know I'm attracted to you. I think you feel it, too."

Gemma shoved her hands into the pockets of her sweater, kept her eyes on the ground, afraid to trust her voice. Every nerve in her body was alive and vibrating.

"I would never hurt you, Gemma."

His soft, tender words only fueled the fears raging inside. "That's what Evan's father said, too."

Memories churned the deep fear to life, constricting her airway. She backed up, pivoted and ran to her car. She didn't doubt Linc meant what he'd said. He wouldn't hurt her intentionally. He would protect her the way he did his family, but she wasn't ready to trust anyone with her heart yet. Not until she could overcome the fear of the past and the man who had caused it. And that might be never.

The house was silent when Linc returned home after the lighting ceremony. He smiled when he saw a foil-covered plate in the middle of the table. Mom had baked cookies again.

Pulling the foil off, he found fresh sugar cookies with colored sprinkles on top. His second-favorite kind. His mom usually started baking Christmas cookies right after Thanksgiving and didn't stop until Christmas Eve. He always loved the way the house smelled during the holidays. At least she was keeping that tradition alive. Linc opened the fridge and poured a glass of tea, then snagged a handful of cookies and headed to the family room. Settled in the leather recliner, he reached for the remote, then changed his mind. His thoughts were too muddled to focus on the television.

He picked up a cookie, the green sprinkles on the top reminding him of how Gemma's eyes had sparkled with the glow of the lights. They had come on in a blaze of glory. The oohs and aahs from the crowd had filled the air and infused him with a swell of pride. Gemma had created an event that shouted the glory of the Lord.

He rubbed the bridge of his nose, aware of the crease in his brow. He was scowling again.

He hadn't meant to kiss her. His only intention was to be together in the carriage and enjoy the lights. But with her at his side and bathed in the warm glow of thousands of Christmas lights, his resolve had crumbled. She'd looked so incredibly beautiful in the soft light, with the colors playing across her hair and reflecting in her pretty eyes.

He'd been powerless to stop himself. He'd spent too much time wanting to kiss her, wondering what it would be like. And he hadn't been disappointed. She'd been sweet and warm in his arms. Holding her had touched a place deep in his core and released dreams he'd buried long ago.

He wouldn't have been surprised if his impulsiveness had earned him a slap in the face, or verbal dressing-down. But he hadn't expected to see fear in her eyes. One moment she was soft and willing under his kiss, the next rigid with fear. It didn't make any sense. For a moment he'd thought maybe she didn't welcome his attention. But he knew better. He knew she felt the electricity racing between them when they were together. The kiss, brief as it had been, had confirmed that. But she was either resisting or denying it, and he wanted to know why.

The more he knew about Gemma the more questions he collected. Now he wanted to know what caused the fear in her eyes. And he had no idea what to make of her comment about Evan's father. What had happened between them that made her barely acknowledge his existence?

The questions plagued him all night and still circled in the back of his mind the next morning when he pulled up at the cottage. He'd texted Gemma first thing this morning to confirm his breakfast with Evan. He was a great kid. He hated that the ball season had come to an end. He missed having practice to go to. But he looked forward to sharing breakfast together.

Linc reached for the door handle to exit the truck, but Evan was already bursting through the front door of the cottage. He pulled open the passenger door and scooted in, a big smile on his face.

"Hi."

"Hi, yourself. Buckle up."

Evan nodded, fastened the seat belt, his feet bobbing up and down as they dangled over the edge of the seat. "I'm hungry."

"Me, too. I'm going to order a stack of pancakes a mile high with eggs, bacon and maybe some biscuits. How's that sound?"

"Good." His toothy grin revealed his excitement.

Some of Linc's enthusiasm faded. He'd hope to have a word with Gemma this morning, but since Evan had been the one to greet him, he assumed she was avoiding him.

The Magnolia Diner was busy but not full. Shirley, the owner for as long as he could remember, seated them at a booth along the front window. Not the same one he and his father had used, but close enough. Linc focused his attention on the last booth, his throat aching at the sight. But the longer he looked, the more memories he brought to mind and the less it hurt. Gemma's suggestion might have been the best advice he'd gotten in a while. It would be easier to come here the next time.

His gaze drifted to the activity outside the window. The city was lit by sunlight now, but traces of last night's grand lighting were still evident. The food vendors' small trailers were closed, but they would open at noon. The horse-drawn carriage passed by with early risers taking in the charm of Dover. Gemma had done a fantastic job and he was so proud of her.

He directed his attention to his little companion. They placed their order, then settled in. They talked about football and school and the Christmas season, and about the "superamazingfantastico" light display his mother had designed. But as they headed home, Evan grew silent and thoughtful, staring out the window. Linc considered prodding him to talk, but decided against it. If the boy wanted to open up, he would.

Linc pulled the truck to a stop at the main house. Mom had texted him that she was home from judging the lamppost contest and to drop Evan off there. They were going to make Christmas cookies for the upcoming community dinner. He'd been invited to help, but he needed to be at the office staying on top of things. Problems were sprouting like mushrooms and he needed to get things under control.

Linc shut off the engine and glanced at Evan. "I had a good time. We should do this every Saturday."

Evan nodded and smiled. "Like you and your dad did?"

"Just like it."

"Was your dad a good guy?"

Linc studied the boy a moment. Where was this heading? "Yes. A very good guy. He was my hero."

Evan lowered his head. "I think my dad was a bad man."

Caught off guard, Linc kept his tone calm and even. "Why do you say that?"

The boy shrugged. "'Cause my mom never talks about him. I don't even know his name."

The urge to pull the boy close was overwhelming, but he resisted. "That doesn't mean he was bad, Evan. Sometimes when parents separate they get angry at each other, and it's easier to forget and just move on."

Evan cast a sideways glance at him. "You think so?"

"Sure. Your mom is a special lady and a great mom. I'm sure she has a good reason for not talking about your dad. She's probably waiting until you're older so you'll better understand."

"I'd understand now."

"Yeah, but you know moms. They like to protect us and stuff." Linc gave the boy an affectionate rub on the back of his neck.

"Okay. Thanks for breakfast. Can we really do it again next week?"

"Sure thing."

Linc watched the boy run to the house and disappear inside. He wasn't sure who was looking forward more to next week's breakfast—Evan or him. But now he also had another question to add to his growing list about Gemma. She was so open and giving. Why would she withhold information on Evan's father from him? Didn't she know it was creating stress for the little guy? Maybe he should talk to Gemma about it. Maybe she didn't realize how upset the kid was.

Something wasn't making sense. By her own admission she'd never been married, so that ruled out divorce. Had she used one of the new fertility methods to give birth? So why wouldn't she simply tell Evan how special he was and how she'd chosen to have him?

He put the truck in Reverse and backed around. But that scenario didn't track with what he knew about Gemma. So what was the story?

He wanted to know, for the boy's sake and for his own, and he planned on asking her at the first opportunity. They'd become important to him, and he wanted to protect them from any pain, past or present.

Chapter Ten

The week had passed with a blur of activity. Gemma strolled down Church Street Sunday afternoon unable to keep from smiling. The streets of Dover were bustling with visitors; the shops around the square had their doors wide-open to welcome shoppers and to enjoy the warmer temperatures that had graced the area this weekend. A sense of pride and satisfaction prompted her to smile and offer up a prayer of thankfulness. Despite the loss of funds, things were still coming together and running smoothly. Visitors were coming to see the lights and seeking out the windows they'd seen online.

This weekend was open house, and the merchants had pulled out all the stops with special sales and prizes. Her part was less stressful this week, mainly to offer encouragement and support.

"Girlfriend, you have outdone yourself. This square is unbelievable." Caroline had joined her today, eager to see all the changes and share in the fun.

"I have to admit there were moments when I didn't think I could pull it all together. Especially after the money dried up."

"You've had a lot of support from the people here.

That's obvious. I haven't seen one empty window on the square."

"Everyone has really stepped up. There were six vacant stores around the square, but the ladies from the library offered to decorate one, the seniors from the community center took another one and various groups finished the rest. I'm in awe of the way people here come together."

"I hate that I missed the lighting event last weekend. I really wanted to see that, but Vince and I had plans. I'll bet it's romantic at night."

"It is. Especially when you ride in the horse-drawn carriage."

Caroline stopped and peered at her. "That sounds like firsthand experience. Tell me you didn't ride in the lovely white carriage all by yourself."

Her cheeks flamed and she tugged her hair behind her ears. "Not exactly." Gemma braved a sideways glance at her friend. Her eyes were wide.

"Who did you ride with? No. I know. Linc, right? I knew it. He's got it bad for you."

"It wasn't like that. He and Francie brought Evan to see the lights turned on and we took a ride around to see how things looked from the carriage. No big deal."

"You are a terrible liar." Caroline nudged her shoulder against Gemma's. "So you said it was romantic. How so? Did he hold your hand, put his arm around you?"

Gemma quickened her steps. She was not going to tell her friend what really happened at the end of that ride.

"Gemma Butler. You kissed him, didn't you?"

Gemma hushed her friend, glancing around to see if anyone overheard. "Will you be quiet?"

Caroline's mouth opened in surprise. "You did."

"Technically, he kissed me."

"And?"

"And nothing. It was just a little kiss." A little kiss that had curled her toes and melted her heart and made her wish it would never end. But she'd pushed him away and ran. He must think she was a nutcase. She'd welcomed his kiss, but the emotions he'd stirred were ones she'd stuffed deep into the back of her heart, never to be touched again.

Caroline shook her head. "Let me guess. You let what happened years ago scare you away."

"You act as if it was nothing."

"You know I didn't mean it like that, but you deserve to be happy, to find someone to love you and Evan, but you won't if you can't let go of the fear and distrust, just a little bit."

"That's not as simple as it sounds." She knew her friend meant well, but she didn't understand. Sometimes having a friend who knew all your deepest secrets wasn't a good thing. They were too quick to hold up a mirror to your faults.

"Well, I think Linc would be good for you. And for Evan."

Gemma couldn't argue that point. Linc would be an amazing father. But that wasn't a future she could afford to entertain. "Speaking of Evan, he's been asked to be the lead in the children's Christmas play at church. He's so excited. He can't wait for Linc to get home so he can invite him."

"Where's Linc?"

"Francie said he's in Louisiana this week on a job. We haven't seen him." Did he really have a job out of state or had she chased him away forever? Maybe he'd decided she wasn't worth the effort.

"You miss him, huh?"

Gemma released a slow breath. "Yes. I'll admit I do."

"I know. That's what happened with me. And look at me now. Vince and I are closer than ever."

Gemma was happy for her friend, but she didn't see any way she and Linc could get closer. There were too many things he didn't know about, and when he did—he'd see her in a different light. Linc was an honorable man. He deserved a woman who was free from shame and baggage. He would never be able to accept her past.

Linc breathed a sigh of relief when he stepped into the large kitchen Monday evening. It felt good to be home. Especially when he could smell his mom's chicken and noodles in the air. His mouth watered. He'd been in Lake Charles, Louisiana, all week dealing with a subcontractor issue on a commercial project. Running Montgomery Electrical was taking a toll. Without Gil to take on some of the problems he was stretched pretty thin.

"Linc. I thought I heard you come in. How did it go?"

His mother came and gave him a hug. "Good. I had to knock a few heads together, though, before they saw reason."

"No one is hurt, I assume." She smiled and lifted the lid on the pot of chicken and noodles. "I hope you're hungry."

"Starved. I'll wash up and be right back." He took a quick shower before going back downstairs. Something caught his eye as he passed the family room. He stopped and stared, slowly approaching the tall flocked tree.

He rubbed his forehead and sucked in a quick breath. No. It was all wrong. He glanced around the room, trying to fit this new object into the old room. "Mom?"

Slowly she came to his side, slipping her arm in his. "What do you think?"

He stared at her, unable to process the change. "I don't know what to think. It's white and covered with glass ornaments and bows and stuff I've never seen before. Our tree never looks like this. It's always green with colored lights and all our old ornaments."

He heard her take a shaky breath and looked down to see tears streaming down her cheeks. "Mom?"

"Every year your father and I were married he always let me do things the way I wanted. Especially Christmas. So when we decorated the tree we did it the way my family had always done. Dale never said a word, never complained. But he told me once that his ideal tree would be white with crystal ornaments and white lights. So this year I put up the tree he would have loved." She sniffed and leaned her head against his shoulder. "I should have done this sooner."

Linc hugged his mom close to his side. "I had no idea."

"Honey, I know all these changes I've been making upset you, but I'm trying to sort out how my life will be from here on. Please be patient."

"You know that's not easy for me." He infused his words with a teasing tone.

"Don't I know it. You're my responsible child, the one who takes charge. Like a sea captain standing at the bow of his ship. Once you set your course you plunge headlong until it's accomplished. I worry that you're missing the joy and beauty around you. You need someone in your life to make you happy."

"I have you."

"That's not what I'm talking about."

"I know." Images of Gemma and Evan filled his mind.

"You need to learn to compromise, son. Be more flexible, pay closer attention to the people and events right in front of you. I know you love the company, but don't let that rule your life. You might miss out on something really important."

"I'll try."

As much as he tried to like the stark white tree in the family room, he just couldn't. He understood why his mom had done it. Though he couldn't imagine his rugged father wanting such a fancy tree. Thanksgiving had been strange without the formal dinner he was accustomed to. Now Christmas would be missing the traditional tree he'd known his whole life. Resentment began to edge out the disappointment. He walked to the window. The lights were on at Gemma's. Maybe she could help him see things more clearly. Odd how he'd never wanted to talk about things until she'd moved in.

He decided not to call to tell her he was coming. Better to simply show up. He picked up a couple cupcakes as a peace offering. She opened the door on the first knock.

"Linc. You're back."

Her smile encouraged him. Had she missed him? He hoped so. "Hey, if you aren't busy I'd like to talk over something with you."

"Sure." She took the cupcakes and laughed. "You don't need to bribe me when you want to talk."

Caught. "Okay. I'll remember that next time." He glanced into the living area and smiled. A six-foot live evergreen stood beside the fireplace. "Nice tree. Kind of plain, though. You plan on decorating it?"

"Yes. I haven't had time to buy ornaments yet."

"Looks a bit crooked. I could fix that if you like."

"Great. Evan and I tried but you see the result."

"Coach!" Evan raced into the room and hugged Linc. "Hi. You missed the big dinner yesterday at the school. There were millions of people there. I helped serve and clean up, and guess what? I'm going to be the narrator in the Christmas play. That's the biggest part."

Linc offered his open palm for a high five. "That's cool, buddy."

"Will you come and see me? Will you?"

"Nothing could keep me away. I'll be front row center." Linc pulled out his cell phone. "In fact, I'm going to put a reminder in my calendar right now." He tapped the screen a few times, then showed it to Evan. "See. Now I can't forget."

Evan smiled. "Awesome. It won't be any good without you."

Gemma grimaced. "Well, I like that. I guess that means I can stay home that night?"

"Aw, Mom. You know what I mean. Hey, Mr. Linc, did you see the tree Miss Francie and I decorated? It looks like a giant icicle."

"Yeah, it does. You did a good job."

"You'd better get back to your homework. Mr. Linc and I need to talk."

Linc settled onto the sofa. "So were there really a million people in the high school gym?"

"Not quite, but too many. It breaks my heart to see so many families out of work and struggling."

Linc nodded. "I keep praying that one year we won't have to hold the dinner at all."

Gemma gave him all her attention. "So what's on your mind?"

"That icicle in my mother's house."

Gemma listened patiently as he vented. When he finished, she leaned toward him and rested a hand on his knee. "Change is part of life, Linc. I know it's hard for you, especially since you value control. But your mother is doing what she needs to do to deal with her loss."

"Everyone seems to be doing that but me."

Gemma slipped her small hand in his, infusing him with strength and confidence.

"You will. Give it some time. You have your family. Whether they are here beside you or not, you know they love you. More important, the Lord loves you. Remember, He lost His earthly father, too. He understands your pain. I haven't lost a parent, but you can always come and talk to me."

Her invitation swelled his chest. He longed to pull her close and share every moment of his life with her. The thought sobered him instantly. He wasn't ready to be rebuffed again so soon. His gaze landed on the crooked tree. He pushed off the sofa and stooped down. "This won't take but a minute. Let me know when it's straight."

"Okay."

Linc stretched out on his stomach, unscrewed one of the bracing pins, using his other hand to ease the truck back an inch or so.

"That's it. Perfect."

He scooted out, rolled over and got to his feet. Gemma was grinning. She reached up and brushed his hair, dislodging pine needles. Her touch sent a high-voltage charge through his body. He couldn't deny his feelings anymore. Gemma was the woman he wanted to spend his life with. He felt at home here, with her. He reached out and touched her cheek. "Gemma, I—" Her eyes softened and she leaned toward him. Memory of the fear he'd seen the last time he kissed her washed through him like ice water. He was getting ahead of himself. Time to step away. "I'd better go."

At the door he glanced at the tree again, smiling at the inspired idea that had just come to him. "I know where you can get some ornaments free of charge."

"Where?"

"The ones my mom didn't use this year. I'll bring them back tomorrow."

Gemma smiled up at him. "Why don't you help us decorate? We need a tall person. I'll make chili. I think it's going to turn cold again tomorrow."

"I'll be here."

Linc whistled softly as he walked back to the main house. An urge to jump up and click his heels together washed over him, but he probably would end up in an inglorious heap on the ground.

He couldn't wait for tomorrow night.

Gemma cradled her mug of cocoa the next evening, watching the silly shenanigans taking place in her living room. Linc and Evan were testing the strings of lights for the tree, but somewhere along the way, Evan had decided decorating his coach with lights would be fun, and had wrapped a string of lights around Linc's neck and across his chest, which had unleashed a fit of giggles in her son. The camaraderie between the two was a sight to behold. The sound of Linc's laughter, deep and full, brought a strange rush of tenderness to her heart. He was always so serious—seeing him relaxed and happy pulled her heart closer to that cliff edge.

"Call me crazy, but I thought the lights were supposed to be on the tree."

The guys' laughter died away. Linc unwrapped the string of lights. "Your mom's right. We need to get these on the tree or I'll be here forever."

The idea sounded good to her. Having Linc with them felt right.

Linc, devoid of lights, smiled over at her. "Are you picky about how the lights are placed on the tree?"

"No. And considering how impatient my son is, I think the toss-up method would be best. I'll clean up in the kitchen while you do that, and then help you with the ornaments."

When she returned to the living room, the lights were twinkling and Evan was happily hanging ornaments from the box Linc had brought. Curious about the type of ornaments the Montgomerys normally used, she lifted one from the box. It was a silver laser-cut Christmas tree made from thin metal material. Linc had explained that each of the five children picked a special ornament each year. She couldn't imagine Linc choosing such a delicate item so she guessed this belonged to one of his sisters.

Peering into the box, she was eager to know each and every ornament Linc had chosen since he was a child. She walked to the tree and hung the delicate ornament on a limb near the top. "Which sister picked this ornament?"

Linc glanced at the silver tree. "Victoria. Bethany liked the old-fashioned glass ornaments. The bigger the better. Tori liked the small delicate ones."

"Which ones are yours?" She pulled a colorful antique sports car out of the box. "The symbol of independence and coolness?"

"You think I'm cool? Actually, that's Gil's. He loved cars and trains." He lifted a small squirrel holding a decorated acorn. "Seth liked the rustic outdoors ornaments."

Gemma searched the contents of the box, trying to decide what kind of ornament Linc would choose each Christmas.

"Can't figure it out? You're slipping."

"I will." She peered into the box again, but the only other options didn't fit the confident, masculine man beside her. She had no idea what kind of ornament he would favor.

"Look for anything with a ball or a bat."

Linc reached in and pulled out one wrapped in tissue. When he removed the paper it revealed a small praying Santa ornament. "This one's mine. Surprised?"

Gemma touched it lightly with one finger. "Not really. I know faith is very important to the Montgomery family. That's one tradition we have in common."

"Good to know. It's the most important."

Bored with hanging ornaments, Evan drifted off to his room, leaving her and Linc to finish up. She selected a small football ornament decorated with a sprig of holly that Linc had claimed was part of his collection. "Can I ask you a question?"

"Sure."

"Why haven't you married? You are obviously a family man. Good with kids. Strong in your faith."

"I've come close. I was engaged once, but we wanted different things. It wouldn't have worked. I'm a one-and-done kind of guy. I want to know it's the right one before I tie the knot."

"Is that even possible these days?"

"I believe it is. I take it you don't?"

How could she answer that without getting into her reasons for being alone? "I believe it can happen. I'm just not sure it will for me."

"The trust thing, right?"

Gemma kept her focus on the tree. He'd remembered her comment. What would he say if she told him her story? "It's different for a single mom. I have Evan to think about."

"I never thought about that." He hung a Saints fleur-de-lis ornament on a branch. "I want what my parents had. I'll know it when I find it."

"Then you'll build that house on your land and live happily ever after?"

"That's the plan."

Gemma tore her gaze from Linc's and hung the last ornament, an oddly shaped papier-mâché star, in the last bare spot. She smiled at the childish design, wondering which of the Montgomery children had made it.

"I did."

She jerked to face him. He was reading her mind again.

"I was in third grade and I hated art class. But my mom had been sick that year and I wanted to give her something special, so I dredged up every bit of creativity I could find and that was the result. Pretty pitiful, huh?"

"No. It's beautiful, and I'm sure Francie thought so, too."

Linc tapped the star with one finger, setting it swinging on the branch. "She must have. It's still in the box. So how did we do? Are you happy with the tree?"

"It's beautiful. Thank you for the decorations and the help. And for including Evan in everything."

"Why wouldn't I? I love that kid. His mom is pretty special, too."

"How about you—do you like the tree? Is it the kind you like?"

"It's perfect. It's what we've always had." He smiled. "Now it's Christmas."

"The tree isn't Christmas, Linc. The people are."

Linc faced her, cupping her face in one hand. "You are such a contradiction. You want all the glitz and flash of the holiday, but you never forget the real meaning of it, either. This year has been hard. I can't seem to find a solid place to stand. Except when I'm with you. Then everything becomes clear."

He tilted her chin upward and placed a light kiss on her lips. Her senses blurred into a warm, dreamy fog. She leaned into him, her hand pressed against his solid chest, only to draw back when she heard Evan call out.

"Tell Coach I said goodbye."

She smiled and glanced at Linc. "Bye, Coach."

"Yeah." He picked up the ornament boxes. "I'll take these back to the house. Thanks for letting me help with the tree."

"Are you still upset with your mom for decorating your tree differently?"

"No. It's growing on me. Now that I know it's what Dad always wanted, it's made me take a new look at some of the assumptions I had. Dad always wanted to make us happy. I don't think I ever considered that he might have set his own preferences aside."

"He loved you so much he wanted what you wanted. That made him happy."

"I guess so. Good night, Gemma."

Gemma shut the door, reliving the moment when he'd kissed her. Each time she was near him she took a step closer to the cliff edge. Tonight her toes were hanging over and she was leaning precariously over the rim. She'd avoided any romantic entanglements since Evan was born. It was simpler that way. No questions, no accusations, no condemnation. But Linc was changing all of her ideas and easing her fears. She was falling for him and starting to think of a different future for her and Evan. Linc made her smile. He made her happy. He made her believe.

She gazed at the beautiful tree they had decorated together. Tonight had been one of the happiest in her life. They'd been a family—sharing a meal, putting up the tree. She hadn't wanted it to end. Fixing another cup of hot chocolate, Gemma curled up on the sofa, her gaze going to the paper star and trying to imagine a boy making a star for his mother.

The opening measures of "Hark! The Herald Angels Sing" interrupted her pleasant moment. The name displayed on the screen shattered her peace. Her mother. When she hung up a few moments later, all her joy in the evening was gone.

Her parents were coming to visit.

Chapter Eleven

Gemma toyed with the beads around her neck, trying to keep her fingers from shaking. This was absolutely the longest day of her life and it was only Saturday. She had another day to survive.

Her parents had arrived midmorning at the Lady Banks Inn in Dover. Gemma had suggested a tour of Dover's charming downtown with the futile hope of impressing them with the decorations. They'd barely walked the length of the park before declaring they were tired and returning to the inn to rest before dinner with the Montgomerys that evening.

She'd been relieved. It was the third weekend, when all the events were geared to the children, and while she didn't have any major Chamber functions to oversee, she needed to make sure everything stayed on track.

Gemma sucked in a breath, but it refused to fully expand her lungs. Now she was in the middle of her worst nightmare. She stole a quick glance at her parents seated near the end of the Montgomery dining table. Her father, as usual, sat sullen and indifferent, ignoring the world around him. So far the conversation had been polite, but she knew it wouldn't be long before her mother started

voicing her opinions. Thankfully, Gemma had maneu-
vered things so Evan was seated beside Francie at the
other end of the long table and not his grandmother.

Focusing her eyes on her plate, she moved the food
around with her fork. Eating was impossible. Giving up,
she clasped her hands tightly in her lap. Every nerve in
her body screamed to take Evan and run to the cottage
and hide until her parents left. A childish impulse, but
she couldn't even face Francie right now, and she wished
Linc wasn't sitting next to her. *Please, Lord, give me
strength to get through this.* Her parents would be leaving tomorrow afternoon. All she had to do was hang on.

"I'm curious, Mrs. Montgomery, what prompted you
to offer my daughter a job decorating your little village? It
seems such a menial task for someone with her intellect."

Here it comes. Gemma's insides plummeted to the pit
of her stomach. Every inch of her skin burned with hu-
miliation. She clasped her hands together in her lap until
they grew cold from lack of blood flow. If only she could
make herself invisible.

Francie gave her mother a gracious smile. "I agree.
Your daughter is very bright, but she's also very talented.
She helped me with a project at the shop and I was im-
pressed with her creativity. I knew she was the perfect
person to take over my role as Christmas chairman."

Arlene Butler took a tiny bite of her roast and nodded. "That was very thoughtful of you, but her father
and I believe she's capable of much more. Beatrice has
recently earned her doctorate in behavioral psychology.
We're very proud of her accomplishments."

Francie smiled warmly at Beatrice. "Congratulations."

Gemma glanced at her sister, who'd been silent
throughout the meal. Beatrice looked years older, sad
and lacking any spark. The realization chilled her blood.

Was that what she looked like? Gemma straightened her spine and attempted to square her shoulders. She refused to let her parents do that to her.

"We still have hopes that Gemma will outgrow this hobby of hers and start another business. One that will succeed this time."

"I believe failure is often the way we learn. My father-in-law failed twice starting Montgomery Electrical. Now we're one of the largest contractors in the South."

Arlene took a sip of her water. "But yours is a legitimate business. Not a hobby."

Gemma spoke without thinking. "It's not a hobby, Mother. It's my career."

"A career that failed because of your poor judgment when it comes to people and your insistence on pursuing a frivolous occupation. How can you make a name for yourself putting together parties?"

"I like my job. It makes me happy. I make others happy. I create memories for them to cherish forever." Inwardly she cringed at how weak and pathetic her voice sounded. Worse still, her comment would only send her mother off on another tirade.

"Honestly, Gemma, what possible good can you do by putting up lights. And in a town this size? There are dozens of companies that could use your abilities. At least *there* you could be making a difference."

Her mother's criticisms were always spoken in a soft, gentle tone, but that didn't lesson the sting. Gemma knew exactly what she was saying. She wasn't good enough. She pressed her hands to her stomach, hoping to quell the churning inside.

She was vaguely aware of Linc shifting in his chair beside her. She started when he spoke. His deep voice commanded attention.

"Gemma *has* made a difference, Mrs. Butler. In fact, Gemma has worked wonders in the short time she was given. She's organized four spectacular events with little more than her imagination and enthusiasm. Her ideas have transformed this town and the way it sees itself for the holidays. I was a skeptic, but she's even won me over. Your daughter has a special gift. A God-given talent, and she's used it to keep Dover thriving. The world may not take notice of what she's done here, but I believe working at the grassroots level is the most important kind of help a person can do."

Gemma sat stunned at Linc's passionate defense. She slanted her gaze in his direction. The muscle in his jaw flexed, and he rubbed the thumb and forefinger of his left hand together, which she'd learned meant he was upset.

She managed a smile to let him know how grateful she was for his defense. He lowered his hand beneath the table, reached over and squeezed her fingers. She grasped his strong hand with both of hers, holding on for dear life.

Francie skillfully steered the conversation in a different direction, asking questions that would afford her parents the opportunity to talk about themselves. Something they loved to do.

After what seemed like an eternity, they announced it was time to leave.

Francie and Linc exchanged pleasantries with her parents, then moved off, leaving her alone with her family. Gemma followed them onto the front porch, eager to say her goodbyes and send them on their way. The forlorn look on her sister's face brought a swell of compassion into her heart. Linc's support gave her the courage to offer her parents an invitation.

"Evan and I are going to church in the morning. We'd love to have you join us."

Her father shook his head. "No interest in that nonsense. We'll see you before we leave."

Gemma knew they would refuse to come, but she'd held out a faint hope.

"I'd like to go with you."

The soft voice jerked Gemma's head around. Beatrice was looking at her with hope in her eyes.

"If it's not too much trouble."

Gemma pulled her sister into a tight hug. "Of course not. We'll pick you up. I'll call you later, okay?"

She bit her lip, the lightness in her chest warming her entire body. Was her sister searching for faith? She prayed she was. She'd watched her today, quiet, submissive, cowed. As if looking into a mirror of what she would have become if she hadn't fought for her own life. Maybe she could lead her sister to the Lord and give her a chance at a new life, too.

"Beatrice. Please get into the car."

Gemma stiffened when her mother approached.

"Your father and I have decided that once you finish this obligation you should come home. We will settle all your outstanding debts and set you up in a business of your own. It's not too late to take the CPA exam and start a real career."

A refusal was on the tip of her tongue. She'd been here before, trying to explain her position, and it always ended in an argument. It was pointless. She smiled, crossing her arms over her chest. "That's very generous."

Her mother nodded in approval, her triumphant smile an arrow aimed at Gemma's heart. It bounced harmlessly off her newfound strength. She didn't wait for them to drive off. She turned around and nearly bumped into Linc. He was frowning again, staring at her with questions in his eyes. Was he feeling sorry for her? Or was he wondering about her mother's comments? Whichever, she wasn't ready to discuss her parents. She forced a smile. "Thank goodness they're gone."

"Gemma, I want to talk to you."

Her throat tightened. She would not discuss her family's dysfunction with him, even if he had defended her. From the look in his eyes, she suspected it was her more personal issues he really wanted to know about and that was not happening. "Maybe later. I'm tired and I need to get Evan home. It's been a stressful evening."

"Sure. I understand."

Gemma hurried inside, thanking Francie profusely for the meal and her tolerance toward her parents' rude behavior. Francie walked her to the door, giving her a warm hug. "We'll save you a seat at church in the morning."

Gemma flashed a small smile at Linc, but didn't linger. She sensed he was full of questions, and she didn't have the strength to deal with that now.

After settling Evan in bed, Gemma made a cup of hot chocolate and settled onto the sofa. She'd feared Evan would slide back into his shell after being with his grandparents, but he seemed fine. Maybe they both had grown stronger living with the Montgomerys.

The winter wind rattled the glass pane in the front window. The weather had turned cold, a nice blessing for the Christmas events this weekend. It helped create the holiday spirit. And would draw more visitors to Dover.

Clutching the warm cup between her hands, her mind replayed the moment when Linc had become her champion. Had he really meant what he'd said? Did he think she was talented, and that she'd transformed the town? She hoped so. His speech had moved her another step closer to falling for him.

Linc was a good man. An honorable and caring man.

But she'd only known him a short while. There had to be other sides to him, like his workaholic bent, and his need to control everything around him. Her heart whispered that he wouldn't try to control her, but her head reminded her that she'd trusted too easily before and ended up scarred and betrayed. Her mother was right about that. She did have poor judgment when it came to her relationships. Where men were concerned anyway.

But if she was going to fall in love with anyone again, it would be Linc. She just wasn't ready yet.

Linc grabbed his jacket from the hook near the back door and started toward the cottage. He wasn't going to get any sleep until he talked with Gemma. He had to understand what was up with her parents. He'd never seen people who were so demanding and controlling. The way they made her cower in their presence made him sick to his stomach. His protective instincts had flared full force, and he'd spoken out in her defense, taking her hand to comfort her and assure her she wasn't alone. The look of gratitude Gemma had given him had made him feel like a knight and pulled his heart even closer to her. But mostly he wanted to know about the offer her mother had made before they left. Was Gemma really considering allowing her parents to set her up in business? The thought of her and Evan leaving Dover left a hollow sensation in his chest.

Hands in pockets, he tromped across the drying grass. The lights were still on in the front room of the cottage, which meant Gemma was still up. His mother had suggested he call first, but Linc didn't want to give her the opportunity to brush him off the way she had earlier.

He raised his hand to knock on the door but hesitated. He wasn't sure what he hoped to accomplish here, but he had to make sure she was okay. He cared about her and he wanted her to know that he was there for her, the way she was always there for him.

He knocked, waving as she peeked out from the curtain in the front room. She opened the door, and like before he was struck by how lovely she was. Her hair was tousled as if she'd run her fingers through it multiple times, and her eyes were red from crying. He resisted the urge to pull her into his arms and hold her close and chase the hurt away.

"Linc? Is anything wrong? Why are you here?"

"I thought you might like to talk. To a friend."

She hesitated so long Linc feared she'd turn him away. Finally she nodded and stepped back to let him enter. The room was warm and welcoming. A cozy fire blazed on the hearth, and the tree he'd helped decorate twinkled like a friendly welcome home.

"Can I get you a drink? Tea? Coffee?"

After getting him a glass of tea, she curled up at the other end of the couch, her toes peeking out from the paisley flannel pants she wore. The toenails were painted green with tiny red stars. He started to ask how she did that but she spoke first.

"I'm sorry about my parents. I should never have agreed to invite them to dinner."

Gemma picked up a large clip from the end table, twisted her long hair into a clump and fastened it on top of her head. He'd seen his sisters do the same thing, only the sight never made him feel warm and soft inside. He had to clear his throat before he spoke again.

"No. It was the right thing to do, but I admit I was shocked at their attitude. I think I better understand some of the things you've said about how you were raised."

"I'm so embarrassed. Your mother has been so kind to

me and Evan, and I repay her by exposing her to my inconsiderate parents." She bit her lip as tears began to fall.

Linc scooted closer and pulled her to his side, letting her rest her head on his shoulder. "No one blames you."

"Thank you for standing up for me. I know you were just trying to help."

Her hand rested over his heart, which was trying to leap out of his torso. "I meant every word. I think what you've done is amazing. In fact, I think you're the strongest, most talented woman I've ever known." He trailed a finger along her jaw and across her chin, ending at the side of her mouth. "I think you're very special."

The fear of being rejected again flashed in the back of his mind, but not strong enough to prevent him from kissing her. He tasted tears on her lips and chocolate. His senses fused into one thought—Gemma was meant for him. She was the woman he wanted to spend his life with. She softened against him, returning his kiss. When he came up for air, her eyes were dreamy. "I think I'm falling in love with you, Gemma."

Her eyes focused, the softness changing to troubled then fearful. "No, you shouldn't do that."

"Why not?" She was pushing him away again.

Gemma stood and walked to the fireplace, staring into the flames. "There's too much you don't know and you'd never understand."

His throat ached at the sadness in her voice. "Then, explain it to me." She shook her head. "I know you have feelings for me. I know you watch me when you think I'm not looking, the same way I watch you. I know your pulse speeds up when I'm close to you. I know you smile when you see Evan and I playing ball."

Gemma glanced over her shoulder at him, her lips

pressed together. "Yes. I care for you. A lot, but that doesn't mean anything."

"Of course it does." He stood and joined her. "Is it because of Evan?"

"Not exactly."

He peered at her more closely. That was an odd response. "Then, what exactly? Help me understand." She turned away, burying her face in her hands. He stepped closer, taking her shoulders gently in his hands. "Gemma, whatever it is, I'll understand. Nothing can be that bad."

Her shoulders arched beneath his hands as she stiffened her spine and sidestepped around his hold. "Yes, it can." She faced him, her green eyes dark and tortured. "I was raped."

Shock jolted through him as if he'd grabbed a live wire. His lungs seized up. He searched her expression, his shock giving way quickly to horror and anger. "When? Who? Tell me and I'll take care of it."

She shook her head. "It was a long time ago. Nine years."

It took Linc a moment to do the math. "Evan?"

She swiped away tears from her cheeks. Nodded. "Yes."

Linc didn't know how to process her revelation. He fisted his hands, fighting the urge to punch a hole in the wall. One look at her filled him with a fierce need to hold her and make the pain go away. He sank onto the arm of the sofa, searching for words that would comfort but needing desperately to know what had happened. "Tell me."

She gulped down a sob. "It won't do any good."

"Please." He watched her emotions scroll across her face—fear, longing, sadness. He ground his teeth together, helpless to do anything constructive for her. Except to pray for understanding and guidance.

"It was my first job after college. I'd been at the company about a year when we started dating. After a few weeks he started pressuring me to sleep with him. I kept telling him I wasn't ready. I wasn't a Christian then. I didn't have a problem with the idea—I just wasn't sure about my feelings. One night he fixed us drinks. I started to feel strange. I couldn't think clearly, my vision blurred. The next thing I remember I woke up in the middle of the night and I knew…what he'd done to me."

Bile worked up into his throat. He struggled to keep his tone calm. "Did you report him?"

"No. He was my boss. I didn't think anyone would believe me. I took a few days off. He wasn't at work when I returned. I learned he'd transferred to the West Coast office. I never saw him again."

"Not even when you learned you were pregnant?"

Tears rolled down her cheeks. "No. I knew he wouldn't want to be involved."

"What about your parents? Did you tell them?"

She nodded, wiping her cheeks. "They were furious. My mother told me I was to blame. She said I must have done something to encourage him. She said I'd ruined my life and no one would want me because I was damaged goods." She bowed her head. "Then she told me to do something about it."

Linc groaned.

"I couldn't. Caroline had just brought me to the Lord. I decided to give the baby up for adoption, but when I saw him, I couldn't do that, either. This precious little baby was mine, and I could raise him in love and happiness. No matter how his birth had begun, I would make sure his life was happy."

She looked at the floor.

Linc hurried to her, wrapped her in his arms, lifting her chin to look at him. "You have nothing to be ashamed of. You were the victim." He brushed her hair off her face. "Ah, sweetheart. You shame me with your strength and devotion."

She shook her head. "I trusted him."

"And he betrayed you." Now he understood why she found it so hard to trust anyone. And why she never talked about Evan's father. How could she explain the violence that had created him?

"I trusted Darren, too, and he stole my business and left me with a mountain of debt. My mother is right. I have poor judgment." She hiccupped a sob. "What's wrong with me?"

Linc held her tighter, cradling the back of her head in his hand. "Hush. I won't let you think that. Your boss was a predator, and Darren was a greedy jerk." The clip slipped out of her hair and fell to the floor, letting her curls tumble down across his arm. "Not all men are like that. You can trust me, Gemma. I would never let anything happen to you."

She slid her arms around his waist. He rested his chin on her head, inhaling the jasmine fragrance in her hair.

"I want to believe that."

"Believe it." He tilted her chin upward, looked into her tear-filled eyes. "You are the most amazing, determined, aggravating woman I've ever met. You make me crazy and happy at the same time." With her wet cheeks and red eyes, she looked sweet and vulnerable, and he wanted to protect her from pain and sadness with every ounce of strength he possessed.

He took possession of her lips, crushed her to him and poured out his heart in the kiss, longing to give her the best part of himself. She meshed with him, returning his kiss with a purity that rocked his foundation.

He sensed her shift in mood. She was pulling away again. She rested her hand on his face, her thumb touching his lip. Then she moved off, picking up the hair clip, turning it over in her hands. "I appreciate you listening, for defending me. That's very sweet. But I'm not ready for anything else, Linc. I can't. Try to understand."

"No. I don't understand. Gemma, let me…"

She turned her back. Shutting him out. His stomach in knots, he pivoted and walked out, pulling the door shut with a bang. Darkness covered him as he walked across the lawn. He welcomed it. It suited his mood.

Gemma walked into Peace Community the next morning with Beatrice at her side. She'd prayed all night that the Lord would touch her sister's heart. The prospect lifted her spirits—but not enough to erase the cold heaviness in her chest that had formed when she'd sent Linc away last night.

"Aunt Beatrice, we always sit with Miss Francie. You can sit beside me so I can show you what to do. In case you don't know."

"That's very kind and thoughtful of you, Evan."

Gemma followed her sister into the pew and sat down, casting a glance around for Linc. Her heart beat triple time thinking about facing him again. She'd agonized all night about how he would feel now that she'd told him about her past. She'd sent him home, needing time to sort through all the emotions reliving the past had churned up. But the moment the door had closed behind him, she'd longed to call him back and fall into his arms again. He was always there to protect and defend her. No one had ever cared enough before.

It was time to face the truth. She'd stepped off the cliff and was in free fall with no idea of her landing spot.

She glanced around the sanctuary again. No Linc. He never missed church unless he was out of town, and she suspected even then he found a place to worship. She admired his deep faith, his commitment to his family. Last night she'd broken down and told him her deepest, most shameful secret. He'd been compassionate, understanding and loving. His kiss had unlocked the last barrier around her fearful heart, but she'd panicked at the depth and intensity of her love for him.

And she worried about how he would feel today, after he'd had a night to consider the things she'd confided. Would he see things differently? Was that why he wasn't at church? He was reluctant to be seen with her now? Her throat convulsed with the thought.

Gemma struggled to keep her focus on the service. She should never have told him. She'd known it would change the way he saw her, but she'd hoped he was different. That he might care enough to overlook her past.

When Pastor Barrett started his sermon it was if he'd known Beatrice would be there today. He spoke of trying to find validation in the eyes of others. When he explained the path to salvation, Gemma noticed her sister brush a tear from her cheek.

Please, Lord, draw her to You.

As they left the church, Beatrice's phone vibrated. Their mother was impatient to leave for the airport.

Beatrice gave Gemma a hug. "This was wonderful. I had no idea church was like this. I have a lot of questions. I wish I could stay longer."

"So do I. You can call me anytime. We can talk. And, Bea, you don't have to live your life Mom and Dad's way. You can strike out on your own."

She looked skeptical. "I saw how hard it was for you. I'm not as strong as you are, Gem. I never have been. And I don't have the support of a family like the Montgomerys or a man who loves me."

"Oh, no, Linc and I are…" What were they now?

"No. He's head over heels. It's in his eyes when he looks at you, and you love him, too. I can see it."

"Maybe. But it's complicated."

"Sis, don't try to control this. Just let it happen."

"I'm not trying to control anything."

"Yes, you are. You think by closing off your heart, suppressing your emotions, you can keep yourself safe from hurt or betrayal. But you can't." Bea pointed a finger at her. "I may not know firsthand about love, but I know you and I know fear when I see it. Linc is a good man. Don't be afraid to let yourself love him. You're happy in this place, doing this job. Evan is happy, too. Maybe someday I can find that kind of joy."

Gemma hugged Beatrice. "I hope so, too."

"We'd better go. Mom will be upset if I'm late."

The farewell with her parents was short and curt. No hugs, no warm wishes. But she didn't expect any different.

She drove back to the Montgomery estate, her heart growing heavier with each rotation of the tires. Had she made a horrible mistake in turning Linc away? Had her fear blocked her from the thing she longed for most?

As she pulled up, she noticed his red truck was missing from the front drive. Further proof that Linc was keeping his distance.

When Evan got an invitation to spend the afternoon with Cody, Gemma went back into town to work. She could not sit home and second-guess her decisions. She had one more weekend of events to oversee, and that was what she needed to focus on. She had to trust in herself and make a life for her and Evan.

Linc braced against the wind that blew across his face, driving dust into his eyes. He squinted, staring at the water rushing past in the streambed. He'd driven out to his land to think things over. But after an hour in the truck and another half hour wandering the property, he was no closer to solving any of his problems than when he'd arrived.

He'd barely slept after Gemma had told him about being raped. He alternated between wanting to wrap her in his arms and keep her safe to wanting to pummel the man's face with his fists. Mostly his heart ached for what she'd endured. The thought of someone violating her, shattering her spirit and her trust left him searching for answers. He'd sent up prayers for wisdom and extra compassion and tenderness to help her if he could. He'd offered prayers of thankfulness as well, that the Lord had brought her through, kept her strong and creative and amazing.

Linc strolled toward the old house. Another problem had plagued him today. One he was struggling with even more. Gemma had pointed out to him more than once that his fierce need to have his siblings in Dover was likely backfiring on him. He hadn't understood. But after seeing the way the Butlers tried to control their daughters—forcing them to follow the paths they thought best and making both women miserable—Linc began to question his attitude. Gemma had fought her way out to earn her own life, but her sister seemed a lifeless shell of a person. He never wanted to control his brothers and sisters in that way—he'd only wanted to keep them close.

The wind made the old wooden house creak and moan.

Echoing the emotions he was battling with. He wanted to preserve the old homestead the way he wanted to preserve the closeness of his family. But he realized now that he could no more force them to follow his wishes than he could force the old house to repair itself.

Maybe his mom was right. It was time to let go of the idea that he was the head of the household and start thinking about a family of his own. It was a dream he'd packed away after his last failed relationship, convinced the pieces of his life would never come together. Then Gemma and Evan had moved into the cottage.

A shadow passed overhead, drawing his gaze upward. The clouds were turning dark, speeding across the sky. The air was thick and oppressive with the high humidity and warm temperatures. A combination ripe for dangerous storms. Time to head home.

Inside the cab of his truck he switched on the radio. He needed to hear some Christmas music to lighten his mood. But of all the songs that could play, "I'll Be Home for Christmas" blared from the speaker, setting his teeth on edge. None of his brothers or sisters would be home for the holidays. He'd held out hope that Seth would be able to come, but he'd called last night and said he had too much studying to do.

The main house was just coming into sight when the music was interrupted with a special bulletin. The cold front barreling through the area was bringing a line of nasty storms, with hurricane-force winds, hail and flooding in low-lying areas. Linc climbed out of his truck and checked the sky again. He needed to get things secured before it hit. And he'd feel much better if Gemma and Evan were in the main house tonight.

After checking with his mom, he hurried to the cottage. Thankfully, Evan opened the door. Linc knew it was cowardly, but he wasn't ready to see the rejection in Gemma's eyes again so soon. "Hey, buddy, you heard about the big storm coming?"

The boy shook his head. "Mom, Coach is here and there's a storm."

Gemma entered from the kitchen as Linc stepped inside. Her shoulders stiffened as she looked at him. "Hello, Linc. What's Evan talking about?"

The cool tone of her voice dashed the last of his hopes. He wanted to believe she needed time to calm down, but from the detached expression on her face, he was getting a different message entirely. "There's a severe storm system coming through tonight. Mom and I would feel better if you and Evan were at the house. With all these trees around the cottage, it would be safer."

"Your mom wants us there?"

Was she wondering if he did, as well? "She's like a mother hen in a storm. She wants all her chicks to be under her wing." He waited while she weighed her options. *She didn't want to be close to him.* His heart pinched in his chest. "It's just for tonight. The weather will clear by morning. Typical for Mississippi this time of year."

"All right. We'll throw some things together and be right over."

"I don't mind waiting to help carry." He smiled, but she didn't smile back.

"We can manage." She made to close the door.

"Oh, okay. Sure." Dismissed. Again. How many times did he need to get knocked beside the head before he got the message? Maybe he'd been fooling himself about Gemma's feelings for him. Could he have misread things so badly, or was he an egotistical jerk who couldn't take no for an answer?

He'd thought he'd found someone he could spend his

life with, a woman he admired, a woman who would be a partner and his friend. Gemma was everything he'd ever dreamed about. He'd never experienced this kind of connection with anyone before. He stopped, turning back to look at the cottage. Realization taking hold. And neither had *she*.

He replayed their last conversation. Fear. That was why she's pulling back.

He knew she cared for him, but she was afraid. The men who had betrayed her in the past had left a deep scar. She saw herself as damaged, worth less than before. Did she think that learning the truth would make him think less of her?

Linc started back to the main house. He knew what he had to do. He had to prove to Gemma that she could trust him, depend on him. In the meantime, a little distance might be wise for both of them. He'd give her time to miss him, the way he was already missing her.

Chapter Twelve

Gemma had never felt so conflicted in her life. Francie had settled them in their rooms at the main house, fed them homemade soup, then brought them into the cozy family room to play a game. Evan had chosen Monopoly. She'd hoped the game would distract her from thinking about Linc, but it had only highlighted the condition of her life. Moving around and around, making some headway only to have someone snatch away everything you'd worked for.

Linc had been conspicuously absent since she arrived. Francie said he was in the study working. Gemma knew better. He didn't want to be around her. What did she expect after literally closing the door in his face?

Still, she was thankful she'd agreed to stay here tonight. There was a fire in the large Montgomery fireplace, the crystal tree twinkled and soft Christmas music filled the room. What more could she ask for on a dark and stormy winter night?

After all, she should be glad she didn't have to face Linc and see the distasteful look in his eyes. He'd been kind and compassionate when she'd shared her shame. But just as she'd feared, her past had shut down any romantic feelings he might have been developing. He was putting distance between them, subtly telling her he couldn't deal with her past.

But she ached to see him, to hear him laugh the way he had the night they'd decorated her tree. She wanted him to participate in the board game, to sit with her by the fire. But that dream was over.

After tucking Evan in for the night, Gemma retreated to her room and prepared for bed. Slipping under the covers, she pulled the blanket up tight around her chin, listening to the wind beat against the windows. The old house didn't budge. She'd wanted to refuse Linc's offer and stay in her cottage, but now that she was here, she was glad she'd come. She felt safe and protected. Or was that because Linc was nearby?

Lightning flashed, illuminating the large bedroom with its antique furniture. A long rumble of thunder ended in a loud crack. It was going to be a long night.

The storm had blown through by the time Gemma woke up the next morning. From what she'd seen from her bedroom window, the trees outside had taken a beating. Limbs had fallen onto the roof of the cottage. Hail had beaten down the shrubs and the ground was littered with branches and leaves.

But the moment she stepped into the kitchen, Gemma knew something more serious must be wrong. Francie's expression was somber and her smile lacked its usual sparkle.

Gemma took time to fix her coffee before asking the question. "How bad was the storm?"

"Pretty bad. Thankfully no one was seriously injured, but there's widespread damage across the town."

"Where's Linc?" She hated herself for asking, but his energy was obviously missing.

"He was up at dawn. A tree fell over at the end of the drive so he cleared that, then took his chain saw into town to see who he could help."

Town. Gemma had a sick feeling in her stomach. "What about downtown? Have you heard how it is?"

Francie slowly set her cup down. "It was hit pretty hard. Linc said to go in as soon as you were up and check things out."

Her throat convulsed, making it impossible to swallow her coffee. "I'd better go."

A short while later, Gemma stood in the middle of the courthouse square fighting back tears. The storm had wreaked havoc on downtown Dover. Lights had been pulled from the fronts of several stores. The giant Christmas tree was still standing, but many of the ornaments were gone. Two of the wreath drapes over the streets were dangling from one side. Power had been out all night and was only partially restored. Tree limbs were scattered throughout the park. One had fallen onto the white tent where Santa held court and had broken the red throne.

She spotted Linc across the park, his chain saw slicing through a thick limb from one of the oaks that hadn't survived the high winds. When he saw her, he shut off the saw and joined her.

"I know it looks bad, but it could have been worse. Don't worry, Gemma. I'll have some of my guys rehang the lights."

She wiped a tear from her eye.

"Mayor Ogden offered as many city workers as we need to clean up. There's no way we can get this all put back together by Friday. It's the last weekend, the one that will highlight the real meaning of Christmas."

She looked at Linc after that speech. He offered a small smile.

"If anyone can get it done, it's you. Let me know what you need and I'll pull some of my guys off other jobs to help you."

He turned and walked away, leaving her with a cold ache in her chest. She didn't realize until that moment that she'd been hoping for a hug, a warm embrace to give her strength and comfort.

A sob escaped her throat. It was hopeless. Everything was ruined. Her special events were destroyed, and along with it, her hope of a second chance at her career. Linc wasn't even going to help. He'd send his crew, but he wasn't going to get involved.

The text notification chimed on her phone.

Saw the storm damage. Time to come home. Even nature is against you. Mom

Her insides collapsed, curling in under the failure. She wrapped her arms around her waist, closing her eyes against the destruction. When she opened them again she was looking at the manger, stunned at what she saw. Amid all the damage, the baby Jesus was right where he'd always been. Solid. Secure. Unchanged.

She took another look around. She knew God had called her to this life—this job. He'd never told her it would be easy. Her gaze landed on the drooping tent and the broken arm of the Santa throne. This weekend was the most important of all. There was no way she'd let those events be canceled, and she refused to allow her mother to undermine her confidence.

If anyone can get it done, you can. Linc's words gave her courage. She was going to prove him right. Another sob coughed out of her throat. "Lord, I don't know where to start. I need Your strength."

She scanned the park and the surrounding buildings. She'd start with the lights. That was the main draw. Everything else she could adjust. But this time, she'd be doing things without Linc.

Slipping her phone into her jacket pocket, she caught sight of a network satellite truck parked at the curb. They were probably here to cover the storm damage for the news. But first, she needed to convince one of the reporters to put her on camera so she could assure everyone that the events this weekend would go on as planned. Raising her chin, she strode forward toward the camera team near the Santa tent.

Linc stared out the window of his dad's office Thursday, willing the pounding inside his head to stop and wishing he could be in two places at once. He wanted to be helping Gemma get the celebrations up and running again. He knew she was crushed by the extensive damage to the square, and he wanted to be at her side to prove to her that she could depend on him. But he needed to be here, too, because Montgomery Electrical was coming apart, and if he didn't do something fast, it would cease to exist.

He'd lost two more bids this week, two other projects were behind schedule and this morning he'd been informed that there was no money left to finish the Coast Line office building in Biloxi. They'd put in a bid that was too low, and if they didn't find the money in the next few days, the company was facing bankruptcy. And it would be on his shoulders.

He'd always been confident in his decisions and sure of his direction. But his world had been spun around in circles and he'd lost his bearings. He'd scrambled all week looking for solutions.

He inhaled a deep breath when he heard the tapping on the office door. He'd called a meeting with Paul Rush, their comptroller, to go over their options. For the next half hour Paul laid out the situation. Dale Montgomery had been good at balancing jobs and bids and cash flow, but he'd been skating close to the edge the last year, counting on future bids coming through. Unfortunately, that hadn't happened.

Linc rubbed the bridge of his nose, his gut twisted in a fiery knot. "What are the options?" Paul shrugged, his shadowed eyes telling the tale.

"Lay off a few people until we can get on solid ground again. Sell off equipment to raise some capital, or shut down completely until business picks up again."

Linc pushed back from the desk and stood, pacing the small office. "I'm not laying anyone off. Not at Christmas. Dad would never do that. Selling equipment won't raise enough money fast enough to meet the draw for the next phase of construction."

He set his jaw. He should have asked for help, involved Gil more in the decision-making process. He'd thought he was prepared to run the business, but he hadn't expected to feel so lost without his father in his life.

Paul tapped the desk lightly. "You should call your mother in on this. Technically, it's her company now."

"No. Not yet. She's suffered enough. She doesn't need this on top of everything else. I'll find a way." Linc refused to let his mother lose her home, or the business. He'd added to this mess. He needed to find a way to fix it.

Paul shuffled the papers on the desk. "We need a huge influx of cash in a hurry. I have a few more options I can look into, but frankly, I'm not hopeful. I never anticipated things going south so fast. Do you have some way to get this kind of money in a matter of days? Legally."

Linc's heart shriveled inside his chest. It was the last thing he wanted to do, but it was his only option. If it saved the company, that's all that mattered. "As a matter of fact, I do." He walked out of the office and headed for his truck. Time to grant an old friend's request.

The Friday-afternoon sun was setting quickly. The long shadows had already darkened the tree trunks along the riverbank. In less than an hour the sun would set. Darkness would block his sight.

Linc faced the front of the old Montgomery farmhouse on his property, his insides tied in knots. In another hour this land would belong to someone else. Instead of becoming his family home, it would be home to a fishing camp. Instead of raising his children on Montgomery land, he'd be telling them how he'd lost it because of his pride and arrogance. He rubbed away the sting in his eyes. Losing this piece of ground would be like losing his dad all over again.

His dad had always envisioned a Montgomery compound. The five of them all living nearby, the grandkids coming around, the family growing bigger and closer. But one by one his siblings were selling off their heritage. Something he swore he'd never do.

But it was a sacrifice he was willing to make to save Montgomery Electric. It was what his dad would have done. The company was their livelihood. It kept a roof over his mother's head; it secured her future. Linc took one last look at the old house, then strode to his truck and climbed in. Heart pounding, he cranked the engine and drove away.

At six thirty, Linc stepped into the law offices of Blake

Prescott. There were a few more details to work out with the buyer before they held the closing. Every muscle in his body ached from stress and fatigue. It had been a hectic week of long days and late nights, all in a desperate attempt to find another solution to save the company. He'd tried every option available, but in the end there'd been only one.

As he took his seat in the small conference room, he couldn't even muster a fake smile as Blake went over the terms to make sure both parties were in agreement. When Blake passed him the first document to sign, a cold chill washed along his veins, making it hard to grasp the pen.

Halfway through the stack of papers, an alert sounded from his phone. His heart died in his chest when he read the reminder. Evan's play. He clenched his teeth, staring blindly at the papers, unable to accept what he was doing. He wanted to bolt from the room. Tell Blake to forget the whole thing. But he couldn't.

"Linc? Everything all right? Is there an error on one of the documents?"

Linc swallowed the bitter laugh that rose in the back of his throat. Error? A big one. And he was making it right now. "No. Just a little cramp in my hand from signing, that's all."

Steeling himself, he scribbled his signature. A half hour later, the sale was complete. He shook hands with the buyer, thanked Blake, then walked outside.

He stopped in the middle of the sidewalk, his gaze skimming over all the beauty Gemma had created for Dover. The lights, the decorations and the tree in the park. He smiled, amazed at her limitless abilities and determination. Not only had she finished everything on time, she'd brought a new level of joy to the town—and especially to him. She'd taught him to laugh again and to see a new vision for his future. One that included her and Evan.

But he knew how she'd interpret him missing the play. It would be a betrayal of her trust in him. Proof that he wasn't dependable.

Tonight he'd not only signed away his past, but he'd lost his future and done the one thing he'd vowed never to do—let Gemma down. He took one last look at the park and the white steeple of Peace Community rising behind the courthouse. Then turned his back and walked away. He'd saved the business, but lost any hope with Gemma. She would never trust him again. Evan would never forgive him.

Gemma glanced over her shoulder once more, watching the back door of the Peace Community fellowship center for a familiar figure. The Christmas play was nearly over. Evan was doing a wonderful job, but she'd seen him glance toward the empty seat beside her, and then to the back looking for his hero. But Linc Montgomery hadn't come.

A kernel of anxiety took root in her chest. She tried to ignore it. She loved Linc, and she wanted to believe he was a good man who could be trusted not to let a little boy down on an important night.

Since the storm, she'd been working round the clock to get things back on track. The TV interview had assured potential visitors everything would go on as planned. It had taken a dozen city workers, many volunteers and a lot of rearranging, but the downtown and the park were bright and shining for the weekend. Linc hadn't been part of any of it.

Tonight the play was open to the public and the church auditorium was packed. This weekend, choirs from other churches would be singing in the gazebo, the mayor would be reading the Christmas story at the nativity and strolling singers would perform all evening. Each of the three churches near the square would be open for prayer or for worship service.

For her, the play was the most important event of the whole month. She took another glance at the door, her heart sinking lower. Pushing aside her disappointment, she focused her attention on the stage and the little boy who would be the star of the evening.

Her eyes grew moist with a swell of pride. Evan was doing a wonderful job. But a part of her heart had gone cold, her hopes disintegrating like flash paper. Linc had proved he wasn't any different than the rest of the men she'd encountered. They couldn't be trusted. She'd been a fool to believe that he was different.

Francie leaned close. "Have you heard from Linc?"

"No."

"He said he'd be here. I called, but it went to voice mail. That's not like him."

Gemma bit her tongue. Yes, it was. She'd counted on him being here for Evan. But she should have known better. She'd trusted her child's heart to Linc and he'd treated it with callous disregard.

As the play drew to a close, Francie started to fidget. Gemma sensed her worry mounting with each passing moment. She understood a parent's worry when they couldn't get in touch with a child. Only Linc wasn't a child. He was a full-grown man who had made a promise and had chosen not to keep it.

The play ended and as the audience stood to applaud, Francie touched her arm. "I'm going to go. I'm worried. Something isn't right. Tell Evan I'm proud of him and

I'll see him back at the house. I made him some special cupcakes."

A lance of fear temporarily pushed through Gemma's anger. What if something *had* happened to Linc? An accident or injury of some kind? The thought left her twisted inside. No. The only thing wrong was that Linc had found something better to do. End of story.

Gemma found her son backstage standing alone. She couldn't tell from his expression if he was hurt or angry. "Evan, you did a wonderful job. I'm so proud."

A smile appeared on his face. "It was fun. Did Mr. Linc come?"

"No. But Miss Francie was here. She said to tell you she's proud of you, too, and she has some cupcakes for you at her house."

"Why didn't Mr. Linc come? He promised." He watched the other kids whose parents were all gathered around. His disappointment magnified her own. She knew he'd wanted to have his hero there tonight.

"I don't know, sweetheart. Maybe he forgot. Or maybe he had something more important to do. It doesn't matter. It's time to celebrate. Christmas is only a few days away. Let's go home and have some cupcakes."

Gemma rested an arm on Evan's shoulder as they left the church. Her anger seethed below the surface as she made a list of the things she intended to say to Linc when she saw him. She'd trusted him.

Her throat closed up.

When would she ever learn? How many times would she have to be knocked down before she accepted that the only one she could count on was the Lord? Everyone else would eventually let you down.

She stole a glance at Evan in the passenger seat. He sat quietly, staring out the window. She knew he was hurting and she ached to fix it somehow. Breaking her heart was one thing. She'd get over that. But breaking her son's heart—breaking his trust—was something she would never excuse. "Are you okay, Evan?"

He nodded.

"I'm sorry Linc wasn't there. It was unkind of him to let you down. I'll make sure he knows how upset you were."

"I was hoping everyone would think he was my dad."

"What? Why?"

"'Cause I don't have one. I just wanted a dad to be there like the other kids have."

Gemma gripped the steering wheel until her fingers ached. If it was the last thing she did, she would make sure Linc Montgomery knew the full extent of his indifference. "Evan. I didn't know you felt so strongly about Linc. But sometimes we make heroes out of people who don't deserve it. And it hurts when they let us down and break promises."

"Coach always keeps his promise. I think something bad happened."

Francie had the same feeling. Was there something to it? "I'm sure he's fine." She couldn't keep the harsh tone out of her voice.

"Mom, are you mad at Coach?"

"I'm upset, yes. He disappointed you. He broke a promise to you, and that's not okay."

"I know. But I still love him. Just like you did me."

"What?"

"Remember when I was at my other school and I got in trouble about my spelling test? You said you were disappointed, but you still loved me."

Gemma's conscience pricked. "That was completely different."

"How?"

Warmth infused her cheeks. How could she explain that failing a test and betraying someone's trust were miles apart? "It just is." She slowed her car as they neared the main house, relieved to find Linc's truck wasn't parked out front. She wasn't ready to confront him yet. She needed to calm down before she lit into him. "Evan. You go on in and get your cupcakes. I need to go to the cottage. I'll be over in a few minutes."

She grasped his hand before he could open the door. "Are you sure you're okay? You're not upset?"

"Not really," he said before running to the main house.

Inside the cottage she struggled with her emotions. Evan was right. And she hated that. Was she overreacting? Or did she have a good reason to be upset? When it came to Linc, she didn't always think clearly. Digging her cell from her purse, she placed a call to Caroline. Her cheery voice when she answered scraped across Gemma's raw nerves.

"You must be a mind reader. I was going to call you in a few minutes. I've got great news. Vince and I are getting married. Gemma, I've never been so happy in all my life."

"That's wonderful. I'm happy for you."

"Uh-oh. What's wrong?"

After some persuading, Gemma filled her in.

Caroline sighed into the phone. "I couldn't come to the play. Was Evan mad at me?"

"No, but he knew you had someplace else to be."

"Maybe Linc did, too."

Did no one else grasp the situation here? "He *promised* my son."

"I get that you're upset, but shouldn't you at least find

out why first? If it were me, wouldn't you talk to me and get an explanation?"

"Yes, but that's different. I thought I could trust him."

"Gemma, you can't keep holding up your past to every guy you meet. There's a big difference between being betrayed and letting someone down. People will always let you down, Gemma. We're all human." Caroline huffed out a breath. "You and Linc are quite a pair. You're both trying so hard to control your lives, and all you're doing is making things more complicated. Linc is determined to keep everything from changing, and you think by distrusting everyone you'll keep your heart safe. I don't think you even trust God."

Gemma set her jaw. "This from a woman who tried to find a man from a list."

"I'm sorry. But I learned my lesson. I woke up and it's time you did, too. I want you to be happy. It's time. Have a little faith."

Gemma ended the call, but was unable to keep her friend's advice from circling in her thoughts like an irritating bug. She hated it when logic and common sense disrupted her righteous emotions. Deep in her heart she knew Caroline was right. It was safer to think the worst, to shove others away and forestall any possibility of being disappointed or hurt. She'd become an expert over the years. But at what cost?

Gemma sank onto one of the dining room chairs, cradling her head in her hands. She would give Linc a chance to explain, and then she'd determine her next move. She owed him that much. She'd do it now and put an end to the emotional seesaw she'd been on. But when she stepped outside, Linc's truck was still absent. She'd missed her chance. Maybe forever.

Chapter Thirteen

Linc knew he was in for one of his mother's lectures when he came into the kitchen Monday morning. He'd arrived home from Biloxi late last night after spending the weekend getting the Coast Line project back on track. With the sale of his property, he'd been able to ensure the completion of the project. He fixed a cup of coffee, then joined his mother at the table, bracing himself for a "talking-to."

He glanced around the room. "Is Evan here? I'd like to talk to him."

"He's in the office wrapping presents," she said, pinning him in place with her stern mommy glare—the one that said, "I know what you did, now explain yourself."

"What you were thinking?"

Linc's confidence shriveled as if he was ten years old again. "I made some mistakes. I had to fix them. I didn't want to worry you."

"That's usually what people say when they know they should have done things differently, but didn't want to face the consequences."

"We lost a couple bids…"

"I know the situation. Gil called and told me everything. Why didn't you come to me?"

Linc rubbed his thumb and forefinger together, searching for the words to make her understand. "I needed cash fast. Everything is tied up until probate."

"Linc, I'm the owner of the company now. You're not solely responsible. We could have found another way. You didn't have to sell your land." She reached over and took his hand. "This isn't the first time the business has been on the verge of failure. You don't remember the bad years, only the good. There are always options, son."

"Gil shouldn't have said anything."

She scoffed and shook her head. "He always tells me things. You're like your dad, keeping everything inside, trying to protect me. I've worried about you. You're so busy trying to take over for your father you can't see what's happening in front of you. You said you felt left out of things. Well, it's because you didn't take the time to listen."

"Someone has to keep family together."

"No one needs to keep this family together." She jabbed her finger on the tabletop to emphasize her point. "We *are* together and always will be. Just because your brothers and sisters are moving away doesn't mean they're taking their love, too. And speaking of love, have you talked to Gemma?"

He blinked, trying to shift gears. "No. I'm sure she's furious because I missed Evan's program."

"I'm sure she is, but that doesn't mean she'll stay that way. Talk to her. Stop trying to control the situation and just tell her how you feel. You've been in love with her from the day she moved into the cottage."

"I do love her, but I doubt she'll even listen to me now."

His mother smacked him soundly on the hand, then pointed at him with a no-nonsense expression he remembered from childhood. It was the same one she'd had when she'd ordered him to go repair the damage he'd caused on a neighbor's property. "It's Christmas Eve. You get up and go talk to her, and don't come back until you've asked her to marry you and she's said yes. Go!"

Gemma sat in her office on the square, tying up a few loose ends from the monthlong events. It could have waited until after the holiday, but she'd been restless and irritable and needed something to keep her busy. Evan was helping Francie with last-minute preparations for Christmas even though it would be a very small gathering. Francie had invited them to spend Christmas Day with them. Gemma had tried to find a reason to refuse, but Evan was too excited. Being near Linc would be torture. He'd been out of town all weekend, forestalling any confrontation. She'd drifted between anger at him for letting Evan down and longing for things to go back to the way they'd been.

Leatha hurried into the office with a conspiratorial smile on her face, bursting with excitement. "You'll never guess what I just found out."

Gemma chuckled. Leatha was Dover's personal Wikipedia. She knew everything. "You'd better tell me before you pop."

The older woman tapped her fingertips together. "I know who paid for all the lights you ordered. I know who saved Dover's Christmas. None other than Linc Montgomery himself."

Her mind skittered to a halt. "Are you sure?"

"Yes, ma'am. My cousin works with the delivery service and he saw the receipt. Apparently, Linc went over the morning after you held that meeting and paid for them. But he didn't want anyone to know."

Gemma blinked and touched her temple, trying to process the information. "Why would he do that? He was against my changes from the first. I don't understand."

"You don't? Well, I do. It's as clear as the nose on your face." Leatha leaned toward her and grinned. "He wanted you to succeed. He cares about you."

Was that true? Was it really because of her? Or had he realized the whole town would suffer if the events failed? No. He *had* cared. She knew that, but also knew her sordid past had proved too much for him to handle. She looked at Leatha and forced a smile. She needed time to think. Alone.

"Leatha, I've changed my mind. Let's call it a day. We can finish up here after Christmas."

"Wonderful idea. I have some shopping still to do." She walked from the office, stopping in the doorway and turning back. "Oh, when you see Linc, tell him I'm sorry to hear about his loss. I know it must have been painful to let it go."

"Let what go?"

"Oh, I thought you knew, you two being so close and all. Apparently Montgomery Electrical was in a financial bind and Linc had to sell his property to save it. Such a shame. That was the first piece of land his great-great-granddaddy bought."

Blood drained from Gemma's cheeks; her chest contracted with such force she couldn't draw breath. No. Linc loved that property. "Are you sure? How do you know?"

"Because my husband's best friend bought it. They signed the papers Friday night."

The night of Evan's play. During the program. He'd

remembered, but he'd had to save his family business. "I had no idea. I'm stunned."

"Well, I'm not. That man is honorable to the core. He'd sacrifice anything for his family." Leatha hurried back to her, wrapping her in a warm hug. "Merry Christmas, dear. You've done a wonderful job here. Dover has new hope for the future. I'll pray your future is equally as bright."

"Thank you, Leatha. You've been a blessing to me."

Gemma held back the tears until she heard Leatha close the front door. A sob, hot and bitter, burned its way up through her chest and into her throat. Helpless against the tears, Gemma laid her head on her desk and cried. Caroline had been right about her—she was afraid to trust anyone, even God. She'd taken matters into her own hands, keeping people at bay, suspicious of every gesture, protecting her heart from any threat of pain. And it had cost her the man she loved.

Tears soaked the papers on her desk. She didn't care. Weak and broken, she turned her spirit upward and prayed. *Forgive me, Father, for not trusting You with all of me—the broken parts, too. Soften my heart. Remove the wall around it. Lord, help me release all my fears and doubts into Your hands. I'm scared to trust my feelings. I love Linc so very much, but I'm afraid I'm not strong enough to survive another heartbreak.*

But I am. And I can be trusted.

Raising her head, she wiped her face with a tissue, a new sense of lightness in her chest. And Linc could be trusted. She'd known it from the start, but the prison of fear she'd locked herself into had been too strong to escape alone. But she was free now and she had the courage to face her future.

Picking up her cell phone, she selected a picture she'd taken Thanksgiving afternoon of Linc and Evan playing ball. Linc had looked at her and smiled. She'd wanted to capture that moment, and the look of warmth and caring reflected in his deep blue eyes. She lightly touched the image with her finger, remembering the feel of his lightly stubbled jaw against her hand. She loved him, and she wanted him in her life. But she'd put so many roadblocks between them, it might be too late.

Today was Christmas Eve. She'd close up things here, then call him and see if they could talk. It was time to step out in faith. Trust the Lord and see how things unfolded.

She'd been a fool. A scared, pitiful fool afraid to trust her heart when everything Linc did and said had proved to her he could be trusted. He would always make sure those he loved were taken care of. At any cost.

Gemma heard the outside door open and quickly gathered herself. "Leatha, did you forget something?" Glancing up, she saw Linc step into her office. Her heart leaped into her throat. "Linc. What are you doing here?"

"I wanted to see if you were okay."

"Why wouldn't I be?"

He shrugged. "You know, the storm and all the damage." He looked like a scared little kid who had to tell the neighbor he'd broken their window.

Her intuition flared again. "Your mother sent you, didn't she?"

He blushed slightly and nodded, slipping his hands into his pockets. "Yes. With very strict instructions."

"Oh?"

He must have seen her love reflected in her eyes because his manner changed. He raised his chin, squared his shoulders and came toward her, confident and self-assured.

He moved closer and perched on the edge of her desk.

"First she wanted to make sure you and Evan will be spending Christmas Day with us."

She nodded, heart pounding. He was so close, she could sense the warmth of him, see the tiny silver flecks in his eyes and the shadows of his lashes on his cheeks. His blue gaze held her captive, making it hard to breathe or even think clearly. All that mattered was that he was here and she had hope. "Yes. We will be happy to fill in for your family again." She couldn't keep the smile from her face.

He leaned closer, stroking her hair tenderly with his large hand. "You and Evan are family. You have been from the first day."

Her mouth went dry from the intensity of his gaze. She stood and moved to stand in front of him, the love in his eyes giving her courage. "Then, why didn't you tell me you bought the lights, and that you had to sell your land?" She laid a hand on his chest. "I'm so sorry. I know how much that property meant to you."

"How did you know?"

"Leatha."

"Right. She's related to everyone in the county."

"Wasn't there some other way? You were saving that for your own family someday."

"I was, but I discovered that holding on to anything too tightly isn't a good thing." He stood and pulled her into his arms. "Something important happened in the moment after I signed my name to those documents. I realized there was something I cherished more."

"What?"

"You. Evan. A future together. Gemma, I love you. I think I fell for you the moment you put me in my place at the cottage that first day. You changed me, changed my ideas of what my life should be about."

"You've changed me, too. I have a new appreciation for family and tradition."

Linc brushed his fingers over her cheek. "I've been looking at tradition as events, things to do. But I realized the only traditions I want to carry forward are the ones my dad gave us. Faith, hard work and being a loving husband and dad. I want to be the man you can trust with everything. I want to be a father to Evan and raise him in the family tradition of unconditional love and understanding."

Gemma slipped her arms around his back, soaking in his warmth and strength. "You are an amazing man." She lifted her face and placed a kiss on his lips, light and tender. She felt his heart beat rapidly inside his chest. "You said there was something else your mom told you to do?"

He smiled, turning her knees to jelly, and she took advantage of the sensation to hold on to him more tightly.

"Yes, but I'll have to show you."

He stepped back and took hold of her hand, guiding her outside and down the block.

He gestured toward the park. "You've done an amazing job. I'm so proud of you. Your events have put Dover on the map. Next year people will come from all over to see them."

"A convert?"

"Yes. You had me pegged a long time ago. The changes— It was too much. Losing Dad, Mom's changes to the family traditions. I never meant to complicate your job."

He stopped in front of one of the empty storefronts at the corner. The local fire department had decorated it with spray snow and painted a winter scene on the glass pane. "I know your plans for the future are up in the air right now. Waiting to see if Dover will offer you a per-

manent job or if a job will open up someplace else but…
I thought this space might work if you wanted to start
a business here. Mom told me there aren't any event or
wedding planners in town. Apparently there's a bigger
market for that kind of thing than I realized."

Linc held her hand, his thumb sliding back and forth
over her skin. "I know the real estate broker. She'll get
you a good deal."

Gemma looked at the window. It was not what she'd
expected him to say, but the idea of staying here in Dover,
near him, was appealing. And she was warmed by his
thoughtful gesture. "It's a good size. But why would I
stay here?"

She saw him search her face, his blue eyes filled with
hope and a hint of doubt. "Because I don't want you to
go." He pulled her around to face him, cradling her face
in his palms. "I want you to stay and give us a chance
to see where our relationship goes. I know you've been
through a lot and we don't know each other very well
and I've behaved like a jerk at times."

"Yes, you have." That brought a smile to his face.

Gemma bit her lip, glancing at the window again.
Francie's real estate sign was in the window. Beneath her
picture was her business slogan. Come Home to Dover.
She belonged with the Montgomerys. She belonged with
Linc.

She faced him, sliding her arms around his neck. "I
think you're right. This would be the perfect place to start
a new business. I even have a name. Gem's Weddings
and Events. But I have one condition." She saw the fear
flash through his eyes. She shouldn't be so ornery, but
she did enjoy keeping him off balance. "The first wedding I plan will be ours."

Realization slowly dawned. A happy smile lit his eyes and melted her insides.

"Gemma." Linc pulled her into his arms, kissing her with all the promise of tomorrow and all the love she'd ever need.

She returned his kiss, releasing her fears once and for all into the hands of the most honorable man she'd ever known.

"I fell in love with you that day you kept your promise to Evan and played ball with him. You made me start to believe I could trust again."

"You can."

"I know." He reached for her again, halting when his text alert beeped. "Mom says come home quick."

The puzzled look on his face gave her a moment of concern. "Is everything okay?"

"Must be." He angled his phone so she could see the big smiley face on the screen.

Rushing home, they found Evan was waiting on the porch when they pulled up at the main house.

He jumped down the steps to greet them. "I didn't think you'd *ever* get here."

Gemma tried to grab hold of her son for an explanation, but he slipped through her fingers. "Why? What's going on? Is everything okay?"

Evan grinned wide and waved them inside. "Hurry up."

The sound of voices and laughter filled the foyer. Linc stopped. "No. It can't be."

Gemma looked to him for an explanation but he only smiled, took her hand and hurried her into the family room.

"Surprise!"

Francie gave her son a hug. "Merry Christmas, dear."

It took Gemma a moment to realize that the people in

the room were Linc's brothers and sisters. She recognized Seth and Tori. The other two must be Gil and Bethany. Gil stepped forward with a smile and a brotherly punch on the shoulder. Linc released her hand to embrace his younger brother.

"I thought you couldn't leave Mobile?"

"It's all over. Abby and I are home for good." He nodded toward the little girl seated near the tree, holding a backpack.

"That's great."

Francie came to Gemma's side, her face glowing with happiness. Gemma took her hand. "This is going to make Linc so happy. He was so disappointed that none of his siblings would be home for Christmas."

"I know. That's why I wanted it to be a surprise."

Linc's delight washed through Gemma like summer sunshine. Seeing him so happy made her happy, too.

A slender woman with flowing dark hair, whom Gemma deduced as Bethany, the dancer, stepped forward and gave Linc a hug. "Hey, big brother. They moved our departure back a few days, so I grabbed a flight and came home. We all need to be together this Christmas. For Mom."

Seth raised his hand in greeting. "I sneaked away, but I have to go back the morning after Christmas." He came and gave Gemma a hug and poked Evan in the chest.

"Gemma, you look positively glowing. Are you in love?" Tori gave her a wink and a quick hug before squeezing her brother's arm. "Linc, I'll be here through New Year's, but then I'm going back. Judy is facing some health issues and I'd like to be there to help her."

A warm tingle skittered throughout Gemma's body as she watched the reunion take place. She knew how much Linc had wanted his family together this year. And now she and Evan would be part of the family, too. She'd truly come home to Dover.

Gil smiled over at her, and she took note of the strong resemblance between him and Linc. "So are you going to introduce us?"

"Oh, sure. I'm sorry." He reached out and drew her close to his side. He rested his other hand on Evan's shoulder. "Gil, Beth, this is Gemma and Evan Butler. My family."

Evan jerked his head around and looked up at Linc, his mouth open wide. "Really?" He wrapped his arms around Linc's waist and hugged tightly. "I wanted you to be my dad."

Linc rested a hand on Evan's head. "That's good, because I want to be your dad."

Francie grinned as her children gathered around Gemma and Evan.

Gemma heard her whisper, "Dale. They all made it home for Christmas. We're together again."

* * * * *

Dear Readers,

Welcome back to Dover for a celebration of Christmas! This book introduces you to the Montgomery family. Five siblings who after losing their father find their lives going in unexpected directions. Linc is the eldest, and he takes his responsibility as head of the family seriously. He's a man who values tradition and keeping close family ties. But holding on too tightly can bring about the opposite result.

Gemma's background is devoid of tradition and family closeness. Both Linc and Gemma have to come to realize that control of our lives, past, present and future, isn't in our hands. God already has our path laid out before us, but we must look to Him for our direction. If we're not plugged into His GPS then fear, obligation and responsibility can become obstacles to the blessing He has in store for us. Linc and Gemma almost missed out on their future because of fear and a need to be in control. Thankfully they both knew where to turn when they were overwhelmed.

I hope you come back to Dover to visit with the other Montgomery siblings and see what challenges they must face before finding their happily ever after.

I love to hear from readers and I appreciate you choosing to read Linc and Gemma's story. You can reach me through my website, lorrainebeatty.com, or write me at Harlequin Reader Service.

God bless.

Lorraine Beatty

COMING NEXT MONTH FROM
Love Inspired®

Available November 17, 2015

A RANGER FOR THE HOLIDAYS
Lone Star Cowboy League • by Allie Pleiter

Ranger Finn Brannigan wakes up in a hospital with no clue who he is. But this Christmas, with philanthropist Amelia Klondike by his side, he'll recover more than his memory—he'll find a love to last a lifetime.

AN AMISH NOEL
The Amish Bachelors • by Patricia Davids

Emma Swartzentruber has been content keeping house for her widowed father—until he announces she must marry. When former love Luke Bowman is hired to revitalize her family business for the holidays, could it be her chance at happily-ever-after?

GIFT-WRAPPED FAMILY
Family Ties • by Lois Richer

Widow Mia Granger is shocked to hear lawyer Caleb Grant say she owns a ranch—and has a stepdaughter. With his support, her bond with Lily grows and Mia realizes opening her heart could mean a new family this Christmas.

THE DOCTOR'S CHRISTMAS WISH
Village Green • by Renee Ryan

When Keely O'Toole becomes guardian to her seven-year-old cousin, she'll look next door to Dr. Ethan Scott for advice. Can the joy of the holidays and one little girl turn these dueling neighbors into husband and wife?

HOLIDAY HOMECOMING
The Donnelly Brothers • by Jean C. Gordon

Former television reporter Natalie Delacroix returns home to be with her family and take a break from her fast-paced life. Instead, she finds herself producing a Christmas Eve pageant and envisioning a future with her high school sweetheart, Pastor Connor Donnelly.

SECOND CHANCE CHRISTMAS
The Rancher's Daughters • by Pamela Tracy

Years ago, a painful tragedy made Elise Hubrecht run from her hometown—and her boyfriend, Cooper Smith. Now that she's back on her father's ranch, could this holiday season be Cooper's new chance with the girl who got away?

LOOK FOR THESE AND OTHER LOVE INSPIRED BOOKS WHEREVER BOOKS ARE SOLD, INCLUDING MOST BOOKSTORES, SUPERMARKETS, DISCOUNT STORES AND DRUGSTORES.

LICNM1115

REQUEST YOUR FREE BOOKS!

2 FREE INSPIRATIONAL NOVELS
PLUS 2
FREE
MYSTERY GIFTS

Love Inspired®

YES! Please send me 2 FREE Love Inspired® novels and my 2 FREE mystery gifts (gifts are worth about $10). After receiving them, if I don't wish to receive any more books, I can return the shipping statement marked "cancel." If I don't cancel, I will receive 6 brand-new novels every month and be billed just $4.99 per book in the U.S. or $5.49 per book in Canada. That's a saving of at least 17% off the cover price. It's quite a bargain! Shipping and handling is just 50¢ per book in the U.S. and 75¢ per book in Canada.* I understand that accepting the 2 free books and gifts places me under no obligation to buy anything. I can always return a shipment and cancel at any time. Even if I never buy another book, the two free books and gifts are mine to keep forever.

105/305 IDN GH5P

Name _____ (PLEASE PRINT) _____

Address _____ Apt. #_____

City _____ State/Prov. _____ Zip/Postal Code_____

Signature (if under 18, a parent or guardian must sign)

Mail to the **Reader Service**:
IN U.S.A.: P.O. Box 1867, Buffalo, NY 14240-1867
IN CANADA: P.O. Box 609, Fort Erie, Ontario L2A 5X3

**Are you a subscriber to Love Inspired® books
and want to receive the larger-print edition?
Call 1-800-873-8635 or visit www.ReaderService.com.**

* Terms and prices subject to change without notice. Prices do not include applicable taxes. Sales tax applicable in N.Y. Canadian residents will be charged applicable taxes. Offer not valid in Quebec. This offer is limited to one order per household. Not valid for current subscribers to Love Inspired books. All orders subject to credit approval. Credit or debit balances in a customer's account(s) may be offset by any other outstanding balance owed by or to the customer. Please allow 4 to 6 weeks for delivery. Offer available while quantities last.

Your Privacy—The Reader Service is committed to protecting your privacy. Our Privacy Policy is available online at www.ReaderService.com or upon request from the Reader Service.

We make a portion of our mailing list available to reputable third parties that offer products we believe may interest you. If you prefer that we not exchange your name with third parties, or if you wish to clarify or modify your communication preferences, please visit us at www.ReaderService.com/consumerschoice or write to us at Reader Service Preference Service, P.O. Box 9062, Buffalo, NY 14240-9062. Include your complete name and address.

LI15

*Amelia Klondike promises to help amnesiac
Finn Brannigan get his memory back. But can they
also give themselves a merry Christmas?*

*Read on for a sneak preview of
A RANGER FOR THE HOLIDAYS,
the next book in the Love Inspired continuity
LONE STAR COWBOY LEAGUE*

"Everything has changed, hasn't it?"

Finn heard the same catch in her tone that he felt in his own chest. He knew he was Finn Brannigan, but didn't know if that was good news. The sense that the life he'd forgotten wasn't a happy one still pressed against him.

"So it's just your name? That's all you remember?"

"And my age." *Tell her you're a Ranger*, the honorable side of him scolded the other part that foolishly refused to confess. It felt as though everything would slam back into place once tomorrow dawned, so would it be terrible to just keep this one night as the happy victory it was? She'd be perfectly entitled to refuse his friendship once all the facts came to light.

Amelia laid her hand on his arm and he felt that connection he had each time she touched him. As if she needed him, even though it was the other way around. "I can't imagine what you must be feeling right now."

The return of his memory was a double-edged sword. "There's a lot floating out there—fuzzy impressions I can't quite get a fix on, but…I can't tell you what it means to know my whole name." He hesitated for a moment before admitting, "For a while I was terrified it wouldn't come back. That I'd end up one of those freak stories you read about in supermarket tabloids."

She laughed. "I can't imagine that. You're far too normal."

Normal? Nothing about him felt normal. The scary part was the constant sense that his normal wasn't anywhere near as nice as right now was, sitting out under the stars near a roaring fire hearing…

Christmas carols. A group of high school students began to sing "Away in a Manger." Finn felt his stomach tighten.

He waited for his unnamed aversion to all things Christmas to wash over him. It came, but more softly. More like regret than flat-out hate. Finn closed his eyes and tried to hear it the way Amelia did, reverent and quiet instead of slow and mournful. Why couldn't he grasp the big dark thing lurking just out of his reach? What made him react to Christmas the way he did?

Don't miss
A RANGER FOR THE HOLIDAYS
by Allie Pleiter, available December 2015 wherever
Love Inspired® books and ebooks are sold.